I0619623

BLACK SCORPION

NYAKNO J. EKWERE

PYXIDIA HOUSE PUBLISHERS

Black Scorpion
Copyright©2020 by Nyakno J. Ekwere.

Request for information on this title should be addressed to
Nyakno J. Ekwere
Email: ekwere007@gmail.com
+234 802 377 9197, +234 703 227 4873

Library of Congress Cataloging-in-Publication Data

Nyakno J. Ekwere
Black Scorpion
ISBN-13: 978-1-946530-25-7 (Paperback)
ISBN-10: 1-946530-25-5 (Paperback)
1. Thriller - Fiction 1. Title
Library of Congress Control Number: 2020947524

Edited by Winnie Aduayi.
Audrey Harrington.

Published in Dallas Texas by Pyxidia House Publishers. A registered trademark of Pyxidia Concept llc. www.pyxidiahouse.com
info@pyxidiahouse.com

Printed in the United States of America

To my wonderful children, Atanganam, Kubiat, Dayami and Akaniyene.

And to all victims of secret cults and gang violence in colleges across the world.

Acknowledgements

Every accomplishment in life is a result of the contribution of many individuals who, both directly and indirectly, share their gifts, talents, experiences, and time with us. This book is no exception. First, I must thank God for giving me the gift of the story.

My heartfelt appreciation goes to my loving parents, Mr. & Mrs. S. N. Ekwere, who exemplify the ideals and nobility of parenthood, raising my siblings and me rightly. Thank you for your support and the principles you portrayed.

My sincere appreciation to my wife and children, who made amazing sacrifices so that I can give my best to the writing of this book; it couldn't have been easy without your understanding and support.

Several friends, too many to mention, took on different roles in making this work a reality; your encouragement and general enthusiasm about my writing made the journey much easier; thank you to every one of you.

I thank the editors at Pyxidia House for their expertise in fine-tuning the ideas and improving the work.

Contents

PROLOGUE

The guard removed my handcuffs, and my fingers clutched the cell bars trying to resist entering what may be my new life. I screeched, rattling the bars, shouting, kicking and trying to wrestle the guards. They tackled me to the ground with some precision punches and kicks, restrained me and threw me into the cell, slamming the gated door.

The prison cell was a hollow cube of concrete and metals, one way in, no windows; it was no brighter inside than the gathering gloom of dusk, even at midday. In there you could have no idea how much time had passed or even if it was night or day. It was totally disorientating by design. Given enough time, a person could forget their own name in there; the isolation was total, and the stimulation was zero. No light, no furniture or cloth of any kind. And nothing to alleviate the stench of festering sewage.

I have to give it to them. This country doesn't just build prisons; they pour pure hatred into the design. My cell was more like a coffin with headroom, enough to lie down at night, curled up like a foetus. The only sound other than inmates banging rhythmically on the thick metal bars was the audio they pipe in from the torture rooms, of which there are many, and the screams were layered one on top of the other, a gruesome choir of pain.

It's 2:00am; it's suffocatingly quiet now. I guess everyone was asleep, including the guards, but I was still awake, staring up at nothing in my dingy, stinky, dark little space, like a caged bird; I kept hearing echoes of the voice of my dear grandpa, teaching me wisdom; he would always say, *"if an action feels as if it comes from your survival drive, with a feeling of pride, malice or fear – stop. But if an action feels as if it comes from your higher thinking mind, with a feeling of peace, kindness and compassion - then proceed."*

But when the dark evil sets its sight on the darkness in its victim with ferocious focus, it does all it can to get the attention it seeks. The dark evil comes at one through one's primitive drive, just like any hunter would aim for the weak spot or moment of an animal, and that was the trouble with me. First, there was a trigger to open up my primitive drive, activate it as fully as possible, then came the impulse to cause harm, one that hurts both others and me. My only protection would have been to run, question my actions, and take full responsibility, for regardless of the evil force, except in the case of true insanity, the responsibility was mine, but I did not do any of that, for I told myself only cowards run and question their own actions; I was no coward, so I indulged myself.

I always had that tendency of misconception arising from my own well-crafted misinformation as a result of my quest to fulfil the exigency of exuberance. This was aptly applied in youthful ambition. Although misguided, I had deemed my action necessary as a necessity toward the attainment of preferences. I always enjoyed and displayed an inordinate desire to perpetually rule my immediate environment through coercion and other unconventional methods. Thus, it had been a long time coming; I unknowingly joined the world of the secret cult in school as a vehicle to my glee.

And even when it dawned on me that it was all too secretly dark, I convinced myself that none of these university secret organisations came about to destroy souls, choosing to be blinded to the "secret" phrase that completes the "organisation". For me, it was simply that deaths arose from attacks which was naturally a domineering principle. Therefore, it's unfortunate that sometimes these attacks led to the loss of human lives, thereby more retaliation and follow-up reprisals.

What I refused to see was the twist in my primitive drive, the quest to blend and dominate: the gains of "blending", if any, were felt by only a select few among us, and I like to say I was one of the gainers, which was all the more intoxicating, albeit fleeting. Other involuntary vices hatched since evil begets evil.

You know, there's a saying that "Man's inhumanity to man makes the angels cry". I would say that it also makes infants slip into a coma; a seizure that definitely returns them to the infernal world. My deeds dragged me this far down. I was only 19 years old; a young man with a full head of hair, six feet tall, light skin-tone, handsome – I had the kind of face that stopped you in your tracks, a charming toothy smile, and of course, my whole life ahead of me. Yet, here I was in this putrid hell.

"Where the hell is Capone? Why is it taking him so long to get me out? I need to get out of this place," I thought. It's been almost one week already; it never took Capone more than a few hours or a day to get us out.

Capone, Etim Nkanta, was the leader of our cult group and the son of an influential, wealthy politician, who got whatever he wanted whenever he wanted it. He supplied most of our weaponry and got us out of every mess, even as Bossman, which made us feel like lords and all the more invisible – we could get away with any crime.

I stood up and shook the iron bars, "Get me the hell out of here," I screamed in anger. But no one came to my rescue after several screams of all kinds of obscenities. When I quietened down, I faintly heard one of the prisoners down the hall say, *"if this boy shout disturb my sleep again, I swear, I go kill am tomoro, make e die. E no know say na here e go end before when e dey kill people for school."*

Go figure, right? I knew better than to keep

screaming; a few days here was more than enough time to understand what happened on the prison grounds. I had seen two persons get stabbed to death by fellow prisoners during the manual labour hours when everyone was let out of their cells to work the grounds. The guards don't care if the prisoners lived or died in here, only that no prisoner escaped.

I leaned back against the wall; it was an absolute waste of time, energy, and even life to keep screaming. Sleep eluded me every night for the past five days I got here: I wasn't even supposed to be at this prison, at least not before I got convicted, which I know I wouldn't – they had no evidence. Rubbing my head with both hands, I slowly slid down to a sitting position, knees folded, with nothing more to do but think and weave through different emotions. I rubbed my hands together in that classic manner villains do; I wasn't about to pretend to be anything other than what I was. Yes, he was right; I did hurt many people in school and while at it, I enjoyed the power. To me, taking more power, making more money, terrorising other students and difficult lecturers were only a game. I made the moves and baited our rivals to make the exact mistake I knew they would; they never disappointed me. My strikes were all variations of

13

the same acts. Any provocation, no matter how small or insignificant, tempers and egos would blow. My signature move was always a solid uppercut to the jaw before I dealt more pain to my victim. Once, one of my unsuspecting victims almost got his tongue cleaved in half by his own teeth. Sometimes, I actually do cringe at the thought of the atrocities I committed, and how it always went unchecked, as I, along with a select few on campus, unleashed terror, unabated, deliberately choosing the path of destruction. I became above the law or better still, lawless, and seemed to get high on another's physical pain, maiming and taking lives with reckless abandon – never convicted. I was bad like that and good like that at my job – I am Undertaker.

A smart man knows not to leave anything to chance, and a hitman understands that any day could be his last; so, seeing the way things are in here, now would be a good time to write to my elder brother, revealing the whole truth.

CHAPTER ONE

Dear Brother,

It is I, Aniete, your younger brother. I thought it best to write, rather than face you when it dawned on me what the verdict of my actions in school might be. Even in writing, it is as unnerving to share these details with you as it is to see the eyes of a vicious snake glaring from a human head; one devoid of conscience – this is how some have described me because of the things I did. By the time this letter gets to you, I may have started serving my prison term, unless I get away free once again as always. This letter may take precisely forty to sixty days or more before you receive it; you know the postal agency in this country is so poorly managed that the parastatal is winning laurels in ineffectiveness and outright failure. Considering that it may take this much time, I have decided to inform you about everything that transpired and led up to this point. My dear brother, Namso, I would tell you the whole truth, some of which would make you cringe, as being deceptive at this point makes no sense.

You are already in the know about my character – bullheaded, albeit mostly misunderstood. So, after digesting this piece, I can only hope that you will learn to forgive me in time. But if you do not, I cannot blame you, for I have brought great shame to the family. My regret no bounds for bringing my dirt to Grandpa's doorstep; I have seen my folly, and my consciousness has awakened. For many nights, my mind kept playing back that night just before I left home to resume university when you and grandpa sat me down advising me about my unusual behaviour leading up to my admission – if only I had known.

The past one year and the many dark memories that followed remain fresh on my mind…

****

The party was in full swing and the hall, dimly lit, was packed with people, and neon lights flashed everywhere like police sirens, but much more colourful. The music was as loud as thunder; it made the glasses on the tabletops rattle. The party was organized by Uduak, Namso's ex-girlfriend; I went on her invitation and insistence. There, I met two young men; they were almost the same age as me, if not older. The tallest among them was Etete, second son of Chief Edem Nyong, the former Commissioner for Finance in the State, while the other was Imoh Utuk, nicknamed "Terror". He was equally tall, but not as tall as Etete, and quite good looking too; he seemed just like the average person you would see on the street. Perhaps, even kinder; he had a lot of friends, male and female, at the party with him, and he paid their bills. Just being around him was like taking a vacation, but he was no open book. Once you got to know him and shared a few more drinks with him, it's too late to back away.

True to his name, Imoh Utuk appeared to be a terror, as he decided who was allowed to sit on our table and who wasn't, and none of the rejected dared argue. We sat facing each other on the same table; we drank, smoked, and got drunk. When the floor was declared open for dancing, Etete and Terror left to dance with their girls while I sat back alone.

17

These two guys had everything going for them, and the clothes they wore made me look down on mine as rags. They introduced me to hordes of girls at the party, and I fell for one, Iniobong. Etete handed out some naira notes to me, urging me to spend and feel free with the girls. Although I was suspicious of them and part of me wanted to walk away, but the level of liquor in my system could not let me focus on common sense; I guess common sense isn't so common after all. One thing led to another, and I ended up passing the night at Etete's house, unknowingly but willingly.

I woke up the following morning, weak and bewildered; the question "where am I?", floated fuzzily in my head. The bedroom was like a perfect magazine cover image – tastefully furnished. The floor was a high-quality, polished wood, dark and free of either dust or clutter, and the couch at the foot of the bed was cream but inlaid with fine green silk. The white curtains were satin, the kind of white that is untouched by hands and devoid of dust, and a cursory look to the right showed the almost hidden cords that were used to open and close them. To my left, there was a big-screen smart television hanging on the wall, and three chairs arranged around the bespoke centre table facing the television. The paintings on the wall were black and white and arranged to look like such done by a professional. Any one of the pieces wouldn't look out of place in the spread of a magazine.

"Was this a dream? This can't be a dream," I murmured.

And while still trying to find my bearing, a dark-skin, petite, pretty girl walked in. She smiled at me; a smile that suggested we had done the forbidden.

"Good morning, Anietie," she said, and then repeated the greeting once more when I didn't respond to her first greeting. "It seems you are troubled?" She enquired.

Indeed, I was. Imagine a poor young man that had just finished writing his first West African Examination Council (WEAC) not too long ago, whom by chance, happened to have met his elder brother's ex-girlfriend, and subsequently, got invited to a birthday party she'd organized for the daughter of a serving Governor in the State. I felt on top of the world, if not honoured. I swore to be there against all odds, and so, I was. Who would not be excited to attend and devour delicacies for free, some that you had never seen, but only heard of? Who would not be happy? I think "happy" would be the right word – to introduce a bevy of lovely girls to a shy, poor fellow like me. Majority of these girls were daughters of prominent individuals in the State. And to think one of these seductive damsels voluntarily partnered with me romantically all through the night was beyond exhilarating. As if that wasn't enough already: Who would not be baffled? Yesterday, I was sleeping on a mat, and 24 hours later, I wake up on a waterbed in a furnished room only fit for a king! I could not believe my luck. I stared at the damsel before me, and in a twinkle of an eye, I snapped back to my senses.

"Iniobong," I said, at last, remembering her name.

"I know you are tired, Annie," she said with an air of satisfied confidence.

"No; I'm not," I lied in pretence to prove my manliness.

"When I came in, you looked lost in thought."

"Yes; I was only thinking about you," I lied again.

"So soon?"

"Yes, of course."

"I see… alright. There's some water for your bath when you are ready," she said, pointing to the bathroom.

"I need to do something about my mouth," I said.

"I know; a toothbrush and paste are in that-"

"A toothbrush!" I exclaimed, surprised, cutting her

off mid-sentence. I had used one toothbrush for more than a year, and because the brush had become too flat to clean my teeth, I had resorted to mostly using a chewing stick.

"I-I-I mean... I'm just surprised you would have a spare toothbrush for me; I never remember to keep a spare at home for my guests," I stuttered, smiling stupidly in defense of my lame surprise at the mention of a toothbrush.

"Typical guy," she waved in dismissal, laughing.

The bed was too satisfying, but I had to get up, so as not to further betray my inner thoughts of awe at such opulence.

She went out promising to be back. A glance at her wristwatch lying on the bedside table reminded me of the appointment I had later with Mr. Agaba, a lecturer in the History Department of the Faculty of Art at the University of Etinan, where I had applied for admission. Although, my encounter with the newfound affluence was worth continuing the experience, but I might not have a second chance with Mr. Agaba, so, I had to get up. It was now a few minutes before 9:00am, and the scheduled time for my appointment was at 11:00am. How many minutes would I spend before honouring the appointment with Mr. Agaba?

Information I heard about him had it that he was time-conscious, and also an incurable disciplinarian. Failure to meet with him would definitely put my quest for admission in jeopardy.

The bathroom was tiled all-white, neater than most rooms that had played host to me in the past; the bath was inviting, and at the same time appeared breakable. I stepped in cautiously; my left foot gave the tub a mark of dirt which got me jolted. Above was a cylindrical container where the warm bath water must be steaming, and an elongated silver tube dangled from the bottom of the container into the bathtub. There was a sign on the handle of the tube which spelt PRESS. I did, and hot water rushed out. Wincing, I stopped the water quickly; it was too hot for bathing, and almost scalded my skin.

"So, there is no cooling mechanism that can change the temperature of this water or what?" I asked myself. "White men you have failed; damn your technology."

After much time spent trying to figure it out, I became furious over another delay and gave up trying. I had my bath under terrible difficulties; the water burned my back mildly. Now neatly wrapped in a giant size towel, I approached a corner of the bathroom where a large dressing table stood with different sizes of cream and lotion containers. A big mirror was framed alongside the dressing table. Combs of various sizes and uses were on there. And brushes of all types were neatly laid out on one side of the large table, all invitingly staring at me. As I stood staring, a thought crossed my mind, and I began to doubt if the occupant of the room was a man at all, maybe an effeminate. Without exaggerating, this corner would compete favourably with beauty salons. I made use of all the cream on the table, in little quantities of each and quickly put on my clothing, set to leave.

Just then Iniobong opened the door and announced breakfast was served, inviting me to join them. Though I wanted to benefit enough from all the luxury, I summoned the courage to resist the offer to avoid being seen or thought of as gourmand. So, I made my way out of the room, declining the breakfast invitation. Was it for good or bad? More of bad because I was hungry, but if this was what it would take to maintain my self-esteem and dignity, so be it. And with that, I walked out of the room into this massive royally furnished sitting room! For a minute, I was lost and stood there, staring like a moron. I quickly snapped out of my moronic state, and then, pretending I wasn't overly impressed with the site before me, I turned left to try to find my way out of the big house, only to come in full view of the dining room overlooking a beautiful well-tended garden. I wish it were just the garden because I would continue on my way out, but the array of food and fruits laid out on the table held me bound and seemed to drag me to the table.

Everyone was already seated on the big dining table with one vacant seat left; I believe it was meant for me. As I gleefully greeted a self-surprised "good morning", sparkling bright eyes on the table turned around, and I instantly became an object of stares. Behold, seated were the Nyongs, including Chief Edem Nyong! I had to personalise the greetings this time, which was to the Chief himself, and his wife, Etete's mother.

Standing face-to-face with Chief Edem Nyong felt otherworldly; we're talking about a man that pulled the strings and called the shots as long as the paraphernalia of government was concerned. It could not have been another person. Speechless before them, I stood there struck, smiling like a fool and overcompensating, which I think they noticed.

But who cares?! I'm standing before a lord with whom anything in this town was possible! And at that, another thought crossed my mind and got me jolted.

Indeed, man is a god, as the good book tells us – an influential god. I was overwhelmed by the influence of the chief, and it felt like I was trapped within an imaginary jail. Etete must have read my mind because like a psychologist, he intervened by loudly dropping the glass of orange juice in his hand on the table without spilling any of it, and everyone's attention shifted to his direction.

Amidst smiles, he said, "Sorry about that. Daddy, this is my friend, Anietie; he is the last son of Dr. Akpabio," he winked at me and continued, "he was also part of the party; I decided to bring him home to say hello to you," he summed up.

"You are welcome, young man," said the chief.

Knowing that his father cherished friends with good academic ambition, Etete continued, "*Em...em*, daddy; he is seeking admission in my department also, but he is finding it a bit difficult: I was wondering if you could help him with that."

My thought exactly! Etete spoke out the very thought that crossed my mind. The night before at the   party, during our conversations, I had mentioned to Etete that I was seeking admission into the University of Etinan, but I didn't know he would try to help me.

Obviously, all Etete's rants about my background were well-dressed lies, but it helped that he did; he made me look like I was all that and more – a right image went a long way with these influential people. So, I just stood rooted to the ground in awful disbelief and didn't say a word.

"You are eating. Have you invited your friend?" Retorted the chief, "Is that how to be a good host?" His father queried.

"Young man, as I said, you are welcome; sit down and eat your food first; do not mind your uncultured friend."

It was only then I realised I was still standing. How could I reject the chief's offer? It was like resisting the supremacy of a deity. I swallowed my unimportant pride and settled into the vacant seat for the sumptuous breakfast with an air of importance. The "son of a medical doctor" indeed! I thought, smiling. At times, it's good to lie; it brought succour and relief where there was none. Before I left them for home, I got a written and signed instruction from the Chief on his complimentary card to take to the Head of History department.

It became apparent that I must assume the role of a son of a wealthy medical doctor wherever I was to be accepted. This was a tasking role as my wardrobe needed a total overhaul. With lean finance, it was clear that this newfound role had some serious implications. First, was that money must be available at all times by all means; failure would be tantamount to murdering of the image.

Anietie! Son of a medical doctor; it couldn't be me – a stack illiterate for a father and a peasant farmer for a mother. What an irony. To say that I was not conscious of where the scenario would lead me to would be downright dishonest because I had seen and heard my likes in such situations and the accompanying nemesis. The money Etete gave me the night before was still intact. At least my day had been made, although one of their drivers offered me a ride as he was taking one of the vehicles for repairs; I declined on the grounds that "I do not want to be caged in opulence. Liberty was a necessity, and I deserved my freedom." Even I laughed at my own excuse: Caged in opulence indeed!

As I hurriedly walked down to the bus stop, pride enveloped my whole being; my head became distended. A bus pulled up, with the Conductor announcing the fare, and of course, the fare was jacked up because of the part of town I was in. It did not deter my ego. Nobody was important to me, and fellow passengers constituted another impoverished community I suddenly couldn't bear to be around for much longer. Thus, I became a *Formula One* driving adviser instantly, barking down orders whenever the driver made a blunder. An older woman who could not tolerate my pomposity rose to the driver's defence, scolding me. Only few people in the bus were my supporters, mostly youths.

"How could anybody blame them? Had they known that I was just coming from Chief Edem Nyong's residence, these wretched souls would have accorded me some respect," I muttered to myself.

Before I alighted from the bus, I ordered the conductor not to collect any money from the three young men who were on my side during the misunderstanding that ensued. When I got down from the vehicle, I paid their fares and told the Conductor to keep the change; this was followed by a chorus of "thank you; thank you." I saw the admiration in their eyes, and I thought, that's what money can do! The role of a medical doctor's son was within reach, and I was grabbing it. What a professional actor I had just become.

Chapter Two

The stairways and corridor of the University Administrative building were crowded with people, and the chaos was so perfect, like a movie. There were the group of new students - "Jambites" they are called, waiting to get registered, lined up on the left side of the corridor, all the way down the stairs, and about ten feet farther down, stood a group of cliquey girls, obviously girls from wealthy homes, and some boys working so hard to get their attention to no avail. There were the old male students who weren't here for anything but to hunt down female Jambites; there were disgruntled students with one complaint or the other about their course grades. And then there was me, not that I fit into any of those groups.

I stood at the corridor in front of Mr. Agaba's

office, watching the chaotic scene around me while waiting for him, armed with Chief Edem Nyong's complimentary card; my golden ticket to admission into the university. The renowned disciplinarian was there, attending to other students. A quick peek at a student's wristwatch beside me put me in the right mood. Though a few minutes behind schedule, I could beat my chest on my punctuality; I was here waiting, and he was busy. After three students had gone in and were attended to, my turn finally came, and I went in. Without much ado, I immediately reminded him of the nature of the appointment and explained my mission, handing him the complimentary card as Chief Nyong instructed. He brought out a pair of binoculars and examined the card, then looked up at me before going through the inscription on the back of the card word-for-word.

"How did you come by this card?" He asked, sizing me up and looking surprised.

"Sir, it's from the Chief," I answered confidently.

"Are you in any way related to him?" he probed, sizing me up again.

"Not really, sir, but we just met and—"

"And what?" He questioned suspiciously, cutting me off mid-sentence.

"Sir, he knows my father, so, when I met him and explained the situation of things to him;

31

he…he… said okay…then...then, he gave me his complimentary card to…to give you," I stammered. But the explanation made sense to him.

I guess Mr. Agaba was surprised to find out that Chief knew me to the extent of attesting for me and appending his venerated signature to that effect.

So, such a little lie can calm tension; I thought. That further motivated me to work on perfecting the art of lying. I must elevate it to another level; my lies must go scientific, for indeed, the whole world was ruled by falsehood.

He brought out a form, tossed it at me irritably, like some powerful invisible force that he could not refuse was forcing him to oblige me. I filled out the required information, and then, he signed it and asked me for my Statement of Result, which I did not bring along.

"Take this to the Dean," he said; "he will tell you what to do."

"Thank you, sir;" I replied.

"Call the next person and close that door very well," he said dismissively.

Beaming with smiles on the joy of such a quick, automatic admission, I forgot to call the next student as I was instructed, but I noticed one of the students knock on the door and went in anyway. I raced down the pavement toward the Dean's office. The Dean was not in, but after waiting a while, as I got up and made to leave, an elderly man walked into the office. I greeted him and stepped aside for him to get in first – a show of respect for an elder. Just then, the Dean's secretary called my attention, gesticulating for me to wait and mouthing, "that's the Dean." So, I sat down again, while she went into his inner office with him; she came out a few seconds later and told me to go in.

"What is your problem, young man?" The elderly man asked, without looking up, scanning through some papers on his desk.

"Please sir, I came to see the Dean," I said, sounding stupid to my own ears. I already know he's the Dean.

"Just to see the Dean?"

"Yes, sir! *Em*.., no sir; I'm from the H.O.D.'s office."

"New student?"

"Yes, sir!"

"No wonder. Ok, here's the Dean, make your request," the elderly man said gesticulating.

"*Em ...em*, please sir, I came to process my admission procedure," I said amidst tension.

"Correct yourself," the Dean barked.

His secretary, whose desk was by his door, heard us and began to laugh. I was ashamed and embarrassed. Since I did not know where I was wrong, I stood there speechless, looking like a moron.

"I said correct your English; this is not secondary school," the Dean repeated.

"I'm sorry, sir, please, I don't understand you," I cried, even more embarrassed.

"What do you mean by saying I came to process my 'admission procedure'," the Dean mimicked, gesticulating wildly.

Human beings are really gifted differently. With all sense of observation, this man was at this instant a professional clown to behold. I had to stop myself from looking amused, lest I mess up my chances here.

"I'm sorry, sir," I said.

"Sorry for yourself," he groaned and took a few steps to the huge mahogany table.

"I came to process my admission," I said finally.

"Your name?"

"Anietie Akpabio."

"From where?"

"Please sir, do you refer to my school or State of origin?"

"All of the above."

"I am from the south, and I attended Community High School, Ikot, Ntok-Eto," I answered with a measure of confidence.

The Dean was writing down the information I gave him.

"Check if I got the spelling of your village name correctly," he pushed the sheet of paper he wrote the information towards me, and I peeped at it, nodding in affirmative.

"Your passport photograph?"

"I'm not with it, sir."

"It's like you're not prepared," he said, looking at me incredulously.

"I'm prepared, sir," I cried, almost weeping. "It's only that I never knew–"

"Now you know, young man; the earlier, the better," he said, cutting me off abruptly.

"Sir, I'll bring it tomorrow–"

"Look, young man," the Dean cut me off again, enraged, "any moment from now I will be–" the doorknob turned, distracting both of us. This singular event cut short whatever the Dean wanted to say.

A young man walked in and greeted us both; he approached the Dean and whispered something into his ear while the Dean kept nodding his big, old head.

The Dean got up as soon as the young man was done whispering in his ears and said, "My friend, I'm off to the union meeting," placing his huge hairy hand on my shoulder, "bring everything that has to do with your admission or else; I will compile the list of admitted students without your name on it and send to the Vice-Chancellor for approval by Friday; you have two days." His index finger was pointing at me repeatedly as he made the statement.

I was short of words; I only managed to keep a straight face.

"Do you understand?" He asked on finishing his threat.

"I do, sir," came my lame reply.

"You had better do," he said with finality.

He walked out with the informant, and I was left with the Secretary, who listed out the needed admission requirements for me. And without being asked, I told the Secretary all the requirements were at home, except a few that I brought. There was no telling the weight of the Dean's threat, so, just to be on the safe side, I quickly dashed home and returned with the entire documents, including my six passport photographs. Who was I to question the institution's infallible authority? To me, as long as they have their say; I would have my way.

"Here are all my papers," I said to the Dean's

Secretary, panting.

She looked at me surprised, taking the papers I handed her and devoted much attention to my Statement of Result.

"You have only four credits," she said.

"No, four credits and three passes," I corrected her.

"Five credits are required; those passes are irrelevant," she said.

"I'm from the Chief," I said defensively, "Chief told me to come," placing the complimentary card before her. "Chief Edem Nyong told me to come that I would be admitted," I further affirmed.

"That means that you have to wait for the Dean to come," she volunteered.

I went outside as she instructed me and settled down on a wooden chair along the corridor. I brought out a leaflet I had received from a fellow student on my way here, inviting me to their campus fellowship. As I glanced through the leaflet, I felt dizzy, and my stomach grumbled from hunger; it was now almost 4:00pm, which was several hours since the breakfast I had at Chief Nyong's house. The scorching atmosphere was now reducing its intensity, and long shadows cast itself on the sidewalk and pavement. Students were still moving around the whole place even though offices were now officially closed. Mixed expressions were ostensibly seen on some of the students' countenance as the returning students exchanged pleasantries on sighting each other. This place must be full of fun; I had to get in by all means: This thought kept ringing in my brain as I sat there waiting for the Dean to return.

"O God, let me be here," I shocked myself with an involuntary prayer.

Just then, an object of fancy attracted my attention; my consciousness shifted to two lizards. One was chasing the other; it seemed all their effort was to steal my attention as they settled before my viewing position to enact mating. Another red neck lizard suddenly appeared, but it was too late; the poor creature had to watch its supposed prized possession satisfying another. What a strange world; I summed up the drama presentation by the reptiles. Life must be survival of the greediest.

I swung from one thought to another until my consciousness was subdued. I must have slept for up to forty-five minutes, when I heard faintly in my slumber, a voice barking, probably at me. I opened my eyes, and right there, was the domineering Dean standing before me. Shame enveloped my entire being; I shyly wiped away the saliva that had journeyed down my cheek to my ear. So, simply put, I had dozed off with an open mouth.

"Community," the Dean mocked, "I thought I was through with you."

"Sir, I came back with those papers that I failed to bring earlier," I explained.

"Come in and let me have a look," he turned the doorknob, and we went in.

"Welcome, sir," the secretary greeted.

"This young man said he'd brought all his papers?" He asked immediately we stepped in without even answering her greetings.

"Yes, sir," she answered.

"So, what were you waiting for then?" The Dean asked, turning his big head toward me.

"Sir; she said I should wait for you."

"Wait for what?"

The secretary brought all the photocopies and placed on the Dean's table.

"Sir; he has only four credits–," she volunteered.

"Four credits and three passes," I interrupted her.

She went on again, "and he said that he's from Chief Edem Nyong," stretching forth her bangle-filled hand to give the Dean the complimentary card.

By this time, I became furious. Who was this enemy of progress that wanted to turn my dreams to nightmares? I seethed within.

"So, you know the Chief?" He asked after reading through the card.

"Yes, sir."

"But you don't merit admission," he stared at me and continued, "I hope he has told you what to do?"

For the first time the Dean wore a smile, and then became more serious again.

"When you bring it, give it to her," he said, pointing at the Secretary.

"Please, sir; I don't understand," I queried apologetically.

"Young man," the Dean went on, "you did not qualify for admission, so, only because the Chief is my good friend; I have decided to do him this favour for friendship's sake. This card was to introduce you to me and at the same time meet up with the settlement, not an outright admission," he concluded.

I think I needed not a soothsayer to tell me his demand. He stood up and prepared to leave, and his secretary started arranging the files. I stood there motionless. It might have been the look on my face that softened his heart. He stopped and his large eyeballs scanned the entire office till he felt satisfied. "My friend," he said, putting his two hands in his trouser pockets, "bring fifty thousand Naira; I will help you out. This is not even enough to stand before the registrar to plead your case, but because of whom you know."

After a long silence, I managed to murmur a defeated thank you.

"Don't mention; you are like a son to me," he brought out his right hand from the pocket and patted me on the shoulder.

"Who is your father?"

"Dr. Akpabio."

"Do I know him?"

"I do not know, sir."

"Alright, my regards to him. Tell Chief that I have done his wish," he said with an air of confidence.

As we were walking out of the office, I looked at the big round clock in the Dean's office; it was five minutes after six. While the Dean and his Secretary walked to a parked Mercedes Benz car, I strolled toward the hostel alone. My spirit became troubled, suddenly nothing was of interest to me, and my conscience was at war within me. I started blaming myself; perhaps, if I had told the Dean that I was prince poverty, son of an honourable wretched man, at least my case would have been considered without any financial obligation. But here I was, son of a phantom medical doctor, a beneficiary of Chief Edem Nyong's largesse; thus, fifty thousand was small money to pay my way through. Where and how I would raise that amount of money compounded my sorrow as the thought of what item to sell occupied my mind.

My poor late father had nothing worth five thousand; a man who commanded respect in poverty. I think he was gifted in that field – a renowned member of the institute of penury. As a level-headed boy of great repute that I was raised and expected to be, to soil my name surprisingly ranked least in my scale of ambition. Does a poor man have integrity? This question was searching for an answer when a car sped up to me. I looked back, and it was no other person than the Dean. He slowed down and beckoned to me, stretching out a stapled paper instructing me to give it to my father. Since I was not interested in any lift of any kind, I rejected his offer to give me a lift home; moreover, his presence was making me uncomfortable. Besides, I wasn't ready to go home anyway; I walked over to a park in the university and sat there to think.

CHAPTER THREE

It was already 8:00pm when I got home, and clearly, there was no food in the kitchen. So, ignoring the gnawing hunger pang in my stomach, I went straight to bed. I laid on my raggedy, flat mattress on the floor restless as I continued to hit solid walls on finding any solution to my problem; I must have finally fallen asleep around 2:00am. Hours later, I woke suddenly, my eyes taking in every ray of sunlight as it streamed through the barred window in the room, the house was quiet, and without a doubt, I knew I had slept too long. The noises outside were of a day in full swing, with blaring horns and loud bus Conductors screaming away their lungs calling for passengers. I looked at the small table clock on the floor beside the window; it was 11.30am. I jumped to my feet, every thought now in high definition; I rushed a bath and got dressed in a fraction of the time it usually took me and left the house.

I walked on with no particular destination in mind; my feet, feeling a bit sore from the impact of the rough path. Each year for the last three years, I have worn this same second-hand Adidas trainers. Once white, they are now rusty brown with dust, but no one ever noticed they were ever white, and the soles were as worn as my own soul feels right now. With each step, I watched the shoelace flop in its random pattern, random and predictable at the same time. I alter each footfall just a little to see the effect just for some distraction, anything that would make me not dwell on my present predicament – where my life was heading without fifty thousand Naira and the possibilities with that same amount. Yet, where would I find that kind of money? I had been walking this dusty path aimlessly for the past hour, unsure of where to go for help. This dust had an aroma of its own and projects a cruel reminder of my poverty-ridden childhood, and possibly adulthood; projecting it so fast that I feared if I looked back at the imprints of my slow steps, it would be too small for the young adult I am and too light for the man I must become.

With that thought playing on my mind; I knew what I must do – I must find the money to buy myself a poverty-free future, and I had only one more day to come up with it. Thus, jolted to reality and filled with sudden desperation, I turned right, running until I got to the major road and boarded a bus to Etete's house.

The Nyong's residence appeared like no one was home, not that it was unexpected; it was almost 2:00pm, but I was willing to wait as long as it took for Etete to return; I didn't have a phone – never owned one, I would have called. I pressed the doorbell and waited, expecting the housekeeper to answer. Surprisingly, Etete opened the door and was quite excited to see me.

"Can you believe he's requesting for fifty thousand Naira," I announced immediately I stepped into the house. "Where will I get that amount of money?" I asked rhetorically.

"Who's requesting for fifty thousand Naira?" He asked, laughing and confused.

"The Dean!" I exclaimed.

"*No mind am,*" Etete said dismissively in pidgin English.

"*See eh, kobo, man no get,*" I responded, slapping my palms together.

"Guy, cool down," he said as if my predicament meant nothing to him.

"Mehn, na, wetin man go do na?"

"Don't worry," Etete consoled, patting my back, "sit down first."

With that, I relaxed on the chair, and Etete threw himself on the sofa opposite me. I knew his criminal mind was planning something sinister if not diabolical; thus, any further interruption was not welcome at this moment. He reached out for the TV remote which lay on the glass-framed centre table and switched on the 75-inch TV. The giant screen lit up the sitting room with children drama from one of the private kindergarten schools; we let it play on as neither of us seemed interested in the programme nor watching TV for that matter. I stared into space periodically, while Etete lay on the sofa thinking and eventually dozed off.

My eyes roamed the sitting room, searching for an object of my fancy. A large framed portrait of Chief Edem Nyong in traditional Efik Chieftaincy regalia hung menacingly. Another photograph of the whole family in a joyous mode hung in a corner above an aquarium. The side of the wall that had the entrance door had a leopard skin on it. I was overwhelmed by the splendour of the room. How could somebody be hungry in this affluence? My imagination began. The rug was soft and soothing, and the split air-conditioning unit showered its coolness down. Within a few minutes of entering the house, the air-conditioning dried up the sweat from every part of my body. Beautiful artificial flowers gave the room a lively atmosphere. The window and door blinds were of satin fabric laced at the top and below, hiding the slide frame of the windows. A Compact Disc player sat beside the TV, high above it was a big oval-shape wall clock that could compete with a bicycle wheel in diameter. On my right were arrays of Iroko-made dining chairs and table; in front of each chair was an upturned teacup on a saucer, and in the centre of the table stood a big chinaware jar of I-don't-know-what content.

At last, my gaze fell on a snoring Etete, with face upward, he dozed like a sleeping dog. I called out to him and informed him about my intention to leave soon as its already dark outside. It was then that he remembered he had somebody with him. Yawning and rubbing his eyes, he got up, apologising to me, as he stretched his lean, tall frame.

"Ekpenyong!" He called out to someone.

I guess the one that was busy all along in the kitchen cooking up a storm, considering the aroma that was coming from that direction. A boy of about 14years came out and announced his presence. "Is there anything to eat?" Etete asked.

"I was just boiling meat to start cooking. But there is that old Afang soup from yesterday in the fridge," replied the boy.

"Warm it for us," Etete said.

My stomach sang for joy at the sound of that. I had not had anything to eat since breakfast yesterday in this same house. The boy turned and whispered greetings to me before disappearing into the kitchen, which I responded by nodding.

The TV screen captured our attention when Etete changed the channel to another station, which was showing a football match between Nigeria and Brazil, a replay of an old game. After a while, Ekpenyong resurfaced with a rectangular tray. The mound of garri sat on the flat plate visibly, vapour rising to the ceiling. My mouth became watery, and I salivated several times before water was brought for us to wash our hands. An eye survey of the soup, with its delicious aroma, forced what was meant to be a thought within me to whisper, "thank God".

The Afang soup coiled itself thick as if competing with the garri. From the sprout cliff, I guessed it had big pieces of meat, four to be precise. The thickness of the soup could easily be compared with Zuma Rock. I believe a seven-month-old baby can sit on it comfortably without submerging. Etete's right hand dived into the handwashing bowl of water and came out just as fast as it plunged in – there was no form of washing by him. I did the same, but my dirty hands had a thorough bath in the water before my eager hand spread its fingers, and a deep patch on the pulverised garri was created. I squeezed and molded it into a ball in my palm, then dipped the big ball into the soup and swallowed while keeping an eye on my tired host.

Etete surprised my imagination. I never thought he would be such a strict adherent to table manners; his ball of garri was quite small, unlike mine, and each ball was swallowed in a sight-to-behold manner – with finesse. Throughout the meal, he ate quietly. Only slight nods of his flat back head whenever I shot a question at him. He devoured the meal absent-mindedly; perhaps, his appetite was lost to whatever was on his mind. Out of the four pieces of meat, he ate only one while my teeth made its way into the rest of the beef one after the other, and thoroughly licked up every drop of soup in the plate.

There was a long silence after the meal. The competition on who will break the silence raged on till I failed unofficially. I finally uttered something, but this Nyong seed was not in the mood to say a word. He stared into space occasionally; his countenance had the picture of a tormented soul. I had a gut feeling he was up to something sinister. Etete had a boyish appearance that portrays innocence to the world, but he was far from innocent; his criminal mind was constantly at war with him. With just a few days of meeting and getting up close with him, I had acquired enough competence to predict his young character.

Anyway, as it is said, procrastination is indeed the thief of time. After several postponements of ideas, including to ask Etete for help with the fifty thousand Naira, my disorganised feeble mind started proffering other solutions to my problems. I could see danger looming if my thoughts were to be taken into consideration; my mind was plotting to steal from some well-to-do neighbours in our area. But I lacked the will power to execute this kind of onslaught on my own. The impression I had was to carry out the theft alone so as to maintain that clean boy image before Etete. The major snag was that I had no arsenal in my armoury, and worse still, inexperience was another factor I had to contend with, which makes me vulnerable. This meant that I could not hide my inability to raise the needed amount from Etete. My newfound friend could at least tutor me on how to raise the money within the short time I had, that is if he could not possibly loan it to me.

While Etete was still staring into space and appeared disinterested in my small banters, I got more serious, "The Dean requested for fifty thousand to secure my admission."

He remained quiet and made no move to respond.

"See... the Dean said I should bring fifty thousand," I repeated.

"Look for money now," he said absent-mindedly.

"For where?" I quickly asked, hoping to get a reasonable reply.

"That's what I've been thinking about."

"Did you also settle before you got into the university?" I asked, since he was in second year. I got a rude shock from the response he gave me.

"Everybody settles these days. There is nothing like brilliance here anymore; this is admission runz. You do yours, and I do mine; they let you in. Yes; we gave them something," he said flatly.

"But fifty thousand is too much," I retorted.

"How much do you have?" He asked, adjusting himself in his seat.

"Mehn; I'm broke," I responded as if I had ever had a dime.

"Do you have anything to sell?" He asked again, now fully interested in my affair.

"*Mehn;* I don't."

"Nothing that is worth up to ten thousand?" He asked.

"For where," I replied.

Minutes later, silence descended again on both of us like people observing a mourning silence for the dead.

"Do you remember that guy that wore baggy jeans with a white jersey of American football?" Etete asked.

"Is it that guy that was following you about?" I asked in response.

"Yes."

"Yes; I remember him. Why?"

"That's Terror," he pronounced the name, beaming with smiles of hope.

"But his real name is Imoh Utuk; *his Dad hold pepper;* very rich man.*"*

From Etete's sudden look, it appeared there was a solution to my cash trap.

"This evening," he continued, "I'll visit him. You

will be coming with me, right?"

"Yes," I quickly answered.

For me, this was another roaming-about; a quest for an elusive admission.

"E-K-P-E-N-Y-O-N-G!" Etete screamed.

"Y-E-S," the boy roared accordingly.

"Go upstairs and look for my black NIKE trainers." The boy rushed up the stairs obediently and began a frantic search for an equally elusive shoe. Immediately, Etete picked the said black trainers under the table and hid it under the sofa he sat on. He then beckoned on me to follow him, which I did. We sneaked into a room that was like a warehouse for the Nyongs. Old and new electronics of different make and models were stacked on top of each other, along with big food coolers, cooking utensils, gas cookers and sacks containing grains of food. He stealthily locked the door against any intruder and pointed his finger at a heap of a box-like object under a tarpaulin. We uncovered it and found four brand new Sanyo air-conditioners sitting on top of each other.

"I will *hell* two of these," he whispered.

"How much will two of these cost?" I asked.

"Mehn, I no sabi; I just need money," he said, wiping sweat from his brow.

"Will this AC be sold at a giveaway price?" I asked in amazement.

"Hold that," he said, pointing at the tarpaulin.

I held it, and he completely removed the white carton containing the new AC, except the top carton. He suggested taking it away from there immediately; then I reminded him of their domestic servant. He tiptoed toward the door and opened it, peeped and gave the all-clear sign. With the same stealth performance, he went to the back door leading to the small garden at the back of the house and opened it, leaving it ajar.

"Brother!" The boy called from upstairs.

We scampered into hiding like rats sensing danger.

"Brother!" The boy screamed again, "it's only the black suede shoe that I saw."

"Search well," Etete countered.

By this time, we had dropped the topmost AC on the floor, the edge pressing my little finger against the floor, which hurt so bad, but I had to play Spartan, enduring the pain while it lasted. A few minutes later, two of the ACs were out of the store resting perfectly under dry plantains leaves outside. Before we headed to the gate to leave for Imoh Utuk's house, Etete urged their house help to relax on the search for the shoe, which the boy gladly welcomed. An *Alalok* – motorcycle rider, approached us, enquiring about our destination. We told him, and the fare we offered was alright for him to also carry the ACs with both of us. So, we headed to Imoh Utuk residence.

In the city of Calabar, motorcycles are the fastest means of transportation. For quick and speedy movements, the *Alalok* played a potential role. The short journey was scary as the cyclist manoeuvred through dangerous traffic. As a *'legsus'* owner, who has perfected the act of trekking, self-esteem was at its peak here. The idea of passing any comment about the risky ride of the *Alalok* man would make me seem like a first timer. To make matters worse, I sat in-between the rider and Etete, lost to defence of any form in the event of an accident, while the rider had the ACs in front of him, sitting on the fuel tank. Anyway, within a few minutes that felt like forever, the *Alalok* rider had sped us to our destination.

Inside, Imoh's compound, we moved swiftly and disappeared into the right-side corner of the building.

"Terror! Terror!" Etete started calling out to Imoh, and finally stopped at the window.

There was silence for a while, then, a male voice

inside the room responded, "Who is that?"

"It I, but you dey craze," Etete responded in pidgin English.

"Oh; Etes man," Imoh exclaimed, raising the curtain on the window to see us; his pimples-dotted face was beaming with smiles.

Then, his eyes caught mine and immediately there was this expression of mild curiosity about me. He waved at me and began grinning from ear to ear again. He spun his right finger around as a signal for something, though I did not understand, Etete did, so I followed his lead. We went around to the main entrance of the big building, and Terror was already at the door. I watched as both rascals were locked in a warm embrace; each time they disengaged, Imoh will yell out Etete's name, and they will lock again. My constantly probing mind went searching for a clue or Terror's source of happiness. Many thoughts surfaced, but none could adequately satisfy my curiosity. So, I gave up and stretched my hand to shake him when he offered his hand.

The introduction was brief.

"This is Imoh, better known as Terror," Etete introduced, though we had met before at the party.

"And you?" Terror asked suggestively.

"I'm Anietie." I simply said, still smiling. Of course,

he remembered me from the party, but he was actually referring to my presence at his house with Etete, which I chose to ignore.

"And me; I'm the greatest guy in the whole universe." The Nyong seed declared, raising his voice and laughing out loud.

"Shut up," Terror said, placing his right index finger on his lips; "it's only in Calabar, not the world," he added, laughing out just as loud.

"No try me...o," Etete warned jokingly.

"This guy is a criminal," Imoh addressed me, laughing and pointing to Etete.

I smiled along as if I was enjoying their drama.

"This is my man, Anietie," Etete said looking more serious now as if to validate my being there with him.

"Anie-hot!" Terror exclaimed, bringing out his hand for another round of handshakes.

Chapter Four

From the expansive and luxurious sitting room, I walked through the corridor leading to many rooms, the last being that of Terror. The door was left ajar. We took off our shoes and entered. Behold, stood a petite brown beauty; a red towel was around her slender frame while she bent to apply some cream on her equally beautiful pair of legs. She turned and greeted us, almost in a whisper. I could see the shyness in her as she became self-conscious, pulling the red towel around her body more firmly. While she was still concentrating on covering her body properly, Terror gave her a sign with his two hands, which I understood, but I guess she didn't. "Edikan, check the fridge and bring those two remaining bottles of beer for them," Terror ordered as if he knew my taste.

The damsel stepped out and returned with two

green bottles as she was told.

"Where is the opener," he asked as she did some frantic search for the opener.

As usual, my eager eyes roved around the room, scanning everything in the process. The thick mattress on the bed was about 12inches high, and beneath our feet was a thick red rug with added underlay. Electronic appliances were all Sharp model. Two movie CDs lay carelessly on the rug.

"My man," Terror said, "don't you want to drink?"

"Ah...ah!" Exclaimed the girl, "don't use your teeth," she cautioned Etete, who had just opened his drinks with his teeth.

The bottle opener was soon found, preventing me from adopting Etete's behaviour. And with the girl within sight, it would have been so demeaning of my fast-rising status, as such acts would be termed uncivilized; I believe cautiousness and good behaviour are attributes of a good home.

We talked for a while from one useless issue to another as I considered them, wondering when we would get to the topic of my pressing issue. Twenty minutes later, Edikan appeared, fully dressed and announced her intention to leave with such pleasure; I hadn't seen a person happier to leave her boyfriend – assuming Terror was her boyfriend. I was especially pleased to see her leave; I was never comfortable with her presence in our midst in the first instant. It was a welcome development for me, even though Etete protested her decision. "You know it's already past 7:00pm and being a girl, she should be at home," I volunteered uninvited.

"Please shun that talk," chipped in Etete.

"Thank you; my brother," Edikan gratefully said to me, "you are the only one that loves me here; don't worry, I will get one of my good friends for you," she added.

"Etete, see your friend…o," Terror said, laughing and pointing at me, "see what he is campaigning for."

"Don't mind them; my guy," she said encouragingly.

"Eddie baby," Etete began, "you are not going anywhere."

"Comot there," Edikan said in pidgin English.

"Don't worry; they are just joking," I said.

"But you have not spent up to three hours here, Eddie," Terror insisted, still laughing.

"No… just say that I've not spent up to ten minutes now," Edikan responded mockingly.

We all laughed, rising to see her off.

"So, Etete, even you don't want me to go, abi? *Na wa for you…o,*" she questioned Etete amidst the laughter.

"I like you; that's the reason why I don't want you to leave now," he defended himself.

"Anietie!" She shouted, turning back to look at me, "I will give you one of my beautiful friends," she said, adjusting a fez cap on her head.

Since I was strolling a bit far behind them, I quickly increased my steps on hearing that and walked up to meet them to join the conversation.

"Which one?" Terror asked.

"Chichi, the Igbo girl," Edikan said, smiling at me.

"What about me?" Etete asked.

"You have one already," she answered.

"Eddie," I called almost in a whisper; "the girl must be as sweet and good looking like you," I suggested.

"Trust me on that one," Edikan boasted.

She moved closer to Terror, and the love birds stretched their talk and cuddling longer than I had imagined, forgetting the rest of us. An *Alalok* that had just dropped somebody pulled up and enquired about our destination; their usual way of looking for passengers. The enquiry was a successful one; Edikan waved at us and hopped on the vacant seat behind the *Alalok*, who wasted no time in speeding away.

We retired back to Terror's room, only for my

heavily burdened mind to embark on a voyage to my village, focusing on my poor mother and her numerous afflictions. A widow whose family-in-law had taken over her poor husband's landed properties, which my father inherited from his father. As her only hope, she laboured to train us through elementary and secondary school, hoping we would also alleviate her situation. Seeing my uncles take away the little we had as if we weren't poor enough already was unforgivable injustice. And then watching my mother toil day and night daily to feed us at least one meal a day, clothe and educate us while she got sick often without adequate medical care due to lack of funds, thereby becoming a shadow of her former beautiful self, was no walk in the park for me; thus, I promised myself that I would wipe away her tears and give her a good life, come rain or shine.

In my early teens, I often had nightmares about her mental state battling against forces bent on sentencing her soul permanently to wretchedness. She seemed to have given up on hope and accepted suffering and poverty as her fate, although her faith constantly blossomed in a great tomorrow for her children – that was her dream. As far she's concerned, her current predicament was only a path, ushering her seeds into financial freedom, which in her mind, would lead to other forms of liberty. My dream had always been to fulfil her dream – to succeed and achieve financial freedom.

"See this guy," Etete's voice pierced through my thought like King Saul's spear in his mad quest to terminate David's life as written in God's Holy book, the Bible.

Etete was referring to my liquor, which was half empty in the gold-rimmed glass. He took it and sipped some of the content.

"So, you haven't finished your drink," he asked, surprised.

Though I had nothing to say, I expected him to understand my situation. The same drink that I used to gulp down with relish was tasteless in my mouth that evening. I looked up, and about ten minutes later or thereabout, I found my hand lifting the half-empty glass of beer to my mouth. Perhaps, that's the only way to clear the doubts that may be playing on my friends' minds about my level of consumption. While I drank up, I caught both of them exchanging furtive glances with each other.

Afterwards, we all sat there, enveloped in silence,

each seemingly lost in his own thoughts, and as the silence grew deeper, I heard my own heart rhythm from within calling my attention once again to my current dilemma; the silence torturing my active mind for a while until the light went off in the room – NEPA had cut off power. This singular act punctured our morbid meditation. Terror got up and pulled the curtains open for more ventilation, and then, we murdered the power corporation with all known adjectives we could think of for such circumstances. It's no secret that the issue of inadequate power supply had been on the centre stage of all regimes in Nigeria, but so far, nothing had come out of the moribund organisation.

"These NEPA people are very stupid," Etete said, fanning himself with a hand-made fan, woven from a palm frond.

"All of them should be killed," Terror added, also keeping his hand busy with a table mat he picked off the table.

"Guy, not that far now... not kill them," I said, laughing, "but see, there is light in all the government officials' houses," I added.

"Yes; that's a well-known secret, and that's why they should be killed; they enjoy steady power while the rest of us suffer for their inefficiency," Terror affirmed.

"These people are a bunch of idiots," Etete retorted as he got up from his seat to take off his shirt, sweating already.

"And it was not quite long power came on, only for them to take it again," Terror said, sweating profusely now.

I have neither known air-conditioning nor fan in my little abode, so the heat meant nothing to me.

"This is nonsense," I managed to say.

"Mehn.., this country and her over one hundred and seventy million people are all crazy," Etete voiced out in exasperation. Just imagine, electricity that is constant elsewhere in some Third-World countries is luxury in this part of our world," he said.

"If I had my way, I would leave this rotten country; I hate it here," Terror hissed, "and there is even no drop of diesel in the house to even turn on the Generator; I sold everything this morning to get some money for my *runz,* and my parents travelled out of the country yesterday. Even the house upkeep money they left, I added it to make up what I needed for my *runz,*" he added, frustrated.

"You will *bone* everybody and leave the country? I asked wide-eyed as if that was all he'd said.

"Bone everybody waka go!" Etete affirmed quickly,

throwing his right hand in the air.

We argued back and forth about leaving the country for a while until Etete had to initiate another topic of discussion. Terror seemed satisfied with this second-round discussion. The university admissions and other abnormally related issues were part of the new topic of discussion. At last, this helped to smoothly usher in our mission, which was laid bare before Terror by Etete, and at that a serious look engulfed my being. Terror was a bit apprehensive; I guess he doubted my ability and resilience. Thankfully, Etete did not labour much to convince his friend, and within moments, hope was rekindled on my admission. The much-needed cash was within my reach only if I would play along, which I was willing to do, and in the process, these brats convinced me that hard work was no longer rewarded in Nigeria. "Everybody is a criminal", they said. And Terror would scream intermittently to give legitimacy to their conduct. "The saints among us are infants", they'd said, and the wild tongues of these cavaliers did not spare even the clergymen. Shockingly, my innocent appearance was a criterion most valued by the duo. "No one would ever suspect you capable of doing bad," they had laughed so hard, "we're on our way to financial freedom," they'd concluded excitedly.

Those two words, "financial freedom" resonated with me, immediately holding me bound like an external force had chained me to an immovable rock, and if I had any doubts about this before, it all bowed and melted away at the sound of those two words.

After much examination, Terror turned and faced me. His vein-filled hands flew toward mine for a handshake. Out of fear of embarrassment and letting down my new persona, I jumped up excitedly, bouncing around on my feet like a ball, and gave Terror a resounding handshake, and at that, I saw what started as a dry smile blossom into a broad smile on his face; this sight gladdened my heart for it confirmed the future was secure for me. Hope began forming in my mind like a foetus in a mother's womb, and all despair disappeared like dew on sighting the sun. For the first time, their useless discussion became appealing to me. Many meaningless conversations came and ended with me participating squarely. Like ice melting on a hot pan, the thought of them being my friends spread all over my body, calming my nerves. But then again, all friendships are based on economic or some more tangible benefit. A mind in despair would never halt wondering; thus, their benefits became a source of worry to me. What do they stand to gain from this friendship with me? And what do I have to offer in exchange for the help they would render? I questioned thoughtfully.

Terror suggested a visit to Udofia, a final year student of Mathematics at the University of Etinan, and a master strategist, as I later came to know. He was always plotting and delivering proofs of success. Udofia was like a godfather on campus, feared and dreaded. The compound, which played host to Udofia was almost adjacent to Terror's house; this was his personal home in the high-end suburb of Etinan, since his family lived out of state; he preferred staying in Etinan during the school long holidays to run his personal business, instead of Port-Harcourt with his parents. However, he also had a small off-campus studio apartment near the University of Etinan, where he mostly stayed when school was in session.

We found other loyal spirits around him on getting to his home, but Terror was the most welcomed guest, which made him grin from ear to ear, savouring the compliments. In acknowledging Etete, he simply flashed an unsatisfied kind of smile at him.

As for me, Udofia spread his strong, long, skeletal fingers around my hand and gave me a firm handshake. His fingers felt like chain bones, whoever he slaps with those fingers was sure to have his jaw dislocated. He came closer and placed his hand gently around my shoulder and jovially advised that I should not be like Etete, who, according to him, was a bloody mugu. As I got to know him more, I came to understand that Udofia's uncomplimentary remark about Etete, albeit jokingly, simply meant that we needed to be more serious and more committed to these deals than ever.

I simply wanted to like him, but I found myself loving him; he was simply adorable, and his father-like nature made it all the more attractive to get sucked into his world. Terror and Etete extended it to worshipping him; Udofia was a problem solver – any problem was solvable with him. Thus, in him, we found solace. Anyway, excited about this business deal we brought to him, which was an opportunity for him to make extra cash, he addressed us by a series of alias, mine was "Sequence"; I guess his discipline suggested most of the nicknames he gave each of us. I gladly accepted my new nickname and told him I loved the name;

it sounded rich and classy, not like those stupid motor park nicknames that those hood rats called one – *Aniii-bobo*, calling it in such local manner.

In my less-than-complicated mind, his desire to know my name was welcome, although I found his rough looks too distasteful, and also intimidating. However, I decided to bury the seeming reservation I had about him for what I believed to be a "brief" period of our acquaintanceship. He and Terror were neck-deep in trying to explain the fine details of the deal to us, and I watched him demonstrating pedantically for clearer understanding. Terror and Etete narrated to Udofia my quest for admission into the university and how the duo promised to deliver as long as I'm willing to cooperate with them, to which they gave him assurance that I was more than willing, and I concurred, sealing the promise to corporate with the words: "Whatever you need me to do; I would do".

All along, Udofia kept his eyes trained on me while playing the diplomat, brandishing an amiable friendliness towards me. And since my friends understood their boss, they all communicated with their eyes, winking at each other each time Udofia had cause to doubt. He soon grinned happily at me, which suggested "welcome" in my head. I commend their effort in my quest to attain tertiary education, but as far as I was concerned, Udofia was beginning to look like one friend too many and my initial love for him was now in full doubt. Etete turned and winked at me. Giving me a thumbs up; he also murmured something like your case is settled. Hearing that, I momentarily pushed aside my doubts and relaxed; I started eating some fried groundnut in my palm that was long presented to us by Udofia.

"Guys, let's be on our way," Terror chuckled as he rose from his seat.

Etete and I rose at the same time too.

"You guys should check on me in three days," Udofia advised.

They both answered in the affirmative, almost together.

I tried to remind Etete that I had only until tomorrow to deliver the money to the Dean, but he said to ignore the timing as that didn't matter; it would be handled. So, I relaxed.

Etete saluted Udofia in a military fashion and Terror followed suit, screaming, "salute to my Capone."

I thanked Udofia in my own gentle manner, as he laughed away those punctilious salutes of the duo,

"Young criminals," he said, searching for pebbles to throw at us.

"Capone himself," they yelled back, taking to their heels.

I jogged up to them at the main road, and they both patted me on the back, signifying all is good now. Udofia was fun to be with, and I thoughtfully shrugged away my doubts; I guess that's his own manner of disguising blending in with strangers.

The town of Etinan was scenic that evening, and the wind was soothing to the skin; it blew ferociously but mild for comfort. Beautiful faces of maidens, walking majestically with an air of sagacity were a great sight for sore eyes; we were marvelled at the sight. The town had this aroma of one delicious scent after the other, all emanating from eateries all around. This seemed to be was a clement haven for any fun-seeking damsel, and many of them poured out into the street this enchanting evening. Terror opted to hang out with us a little longer; perhaps, to chat with any of these girls, but I just wanted to trek back to my place; at least some money would be saved from excessive spending on transportation. Terror was in for it if Etete and I would give our consent, but my near-empty pocket, and my shyness about girls prevented any positive approval from me; I feigned tiredness. Terror stealthily squeezed some naira notes into Etete's left palm for our fare. Then, he excused himself and bid us farewell, but instead of crossing to the other side of the street to his house, he swiftly walked towards the direction of a girl, who had walked past us a few minutes ago. We waited for some time for Terror to fade away with the girl before we picked an *Alalok* to Etete's house. I followed Etete to his house because I didn't want him to see me trekking home, and I had a question for him, anyway.

On getting to Chief Edem Nyong's residence, Etete gave me the balance of the transportation fare doled out to him by Terror; I thanked him. Then as he made to go in, I asked him why Udofia was called "Capone".

"It's just a nickname that suits his profile of being able to fix any problem brought to him, including finding a buyer for anything someone needed to sell quickly for some quick bucks, and of course, his mathematical prowess too; *his head is hot* – brilliant guy! He is a straight-A student; a legit straight-A, not the one people settle lecturers to get. It's just the same way he called you, "Sequence" today, which really means nothing," he explained.

"Why do you ask?" He asked.

"Nothing, just curious; I like the name," I shrugged, bidding him goodnight and thanked him again.

I waited till he disappeared into his house, then I set off on my journey back home with my *legsus,* saving the money for a good meal tomorrow.

CHAPTER FIVE

I sat outside on my doorstep in the warm breeze of the morning yet shivering. My heart was pounding so fast as if it would break out of my chest. I was beyond frantic; it's been two weeks, and I still had no way forward on paying the fifty thousand required for my admission. My mind was in knots as my brain was continually searching for any sign that everything was alright; neither Etete nor Terror and Udofia had made it any easier; they had become almost unreachable; I had no phone to call any of them, so, I could only go to their homes, and the few times I was able to find Etete at home, all he said to me was "relax, we're handling it; you will gain admission".

But how could I relax, the Dean had gone on to submit the names of the admitted students. And my name was not on the list published last week.

I was desperate, too desperate for comfort; we're talking about my future here. My stomach shifted uneasily, and I noticed that the hands that I was hugging myself with were pinching into my skin. I released my hands, but then I couldn't figure out what to do with them, so instead, they clasped and unclasped each other as if in constant need of touch and reassurance. But what they needed was to be able to touch the second list of admitted students on the University Admissions Notice board and find my name on it. I still didn't have the money or knew if my friends got it; I was not even sure if the Dean would still accept the money, since it was long past the due date to get it to him. The suspense, this waiting game, was killing me.

Three weeks later, I finally got some hope from Etete and Imoh Utuk – Terror; they asked me to meet them at Terror's house. When I got to Terror's house, his room looked a tad bit too dark, which made me quite uneasy, so I suggested that I draw the curtains and open the windows to brighten and ventilate the room – there was no power, but he turned me down. Then, Etete took out a black polythene bag and emptied the bulky content on the bed while Terror was unwrapping something from a big brown envelope that he removed from the upper chamber of his cupboard.

I had seen money at the bank severally, but never anywhere else have I seen so many notes of Naira with someone close to me like what I saw on Imoh's bed – well-packaged notes of Naira in 200 denominations. None of them told me how, where, and when they got the money. I suspected Terror must have been in some robbery somewhere; I had never trusted that criminal. The bundles were shared amongst the three of us to count; I was shaky and unfocused. Initially, I had counted N71,000 (Naira), but on the second count, I arrived at 69,000; then Etete assisted me in counting, and it turned out to be N67,000 (Naira). They simply dismissed it as being that I wasn't used to this kind of endeavours. Etete and Terror got N97,000 and N84,000 (Naira) from their own bundles respectively, making it a total of N248,000 (Naira). Terror counted N30,000 from the N67,000 that I counted and gave it to me, and Etete counted N20,000 from his bundle and tossed it to me.

"That's some money to get the personal stuff you need for school; we've already settled your N50k debt for admission *runz*; your name should be on the second list coming out," Etete said, smiling mischievously, and urging Terror to say something. I had not bothered to go to the school to check the second list that was released earlier today since I was sure my name wouldn't be on it, having not paid the required N50,000 for admission. So, I made a mental note to stop by the school and check as soon as I leave this place.

At this point, Terror sat up straight on the bed, looking more serious, and stared at me piercingly as if scanning my brain to dictate elements of treachery in the future.

"Has your guy here informed you that we have decided you would become part of our inner circle of friends… and you have to always look sharp? He asked defiantly.

"Bros, which one na? I'm already with you people, no shaking," I said, jumping up and feigning a boldness that I did not feel as I silently prayed the inner circle did not mean armed robbery; yet, I sought their acceptance.

"Ok o; let it be as you said; no stories later," Terror said, getting up to stretch.

With the mention of the word "inner circle", I had a feeling it was much more than a normal close friendship, but there was no courage in me to resist the offer. This was a war between the future and the present; the choice of university admission would be in the balance with any irrational decision. And this N50,000 would do plenty of good for my poor mother in the village; at least I can send her N25,000 to support them at home and manage the remaining N25,000 for my books and handouts. This was how I reasoned it all and accepted the money, dismissing my concerns.

"You guys are my brothers already; this is much more than friends would do now. You don't know what you have done for me; I'm committed to you guys for life!" I said emphatically, trying to reassure them, while still hoping for the best.

Interestingly, just as I was finishing my last sentence, Udofia walked in. After exchanging pleasantries with the guys, he turned to me, calling me "Sequence" as he'd nicknamed me, in a tone filled with meaning, but I could not decipher, and with his eyes still trained on me, he said he was there to see me and deliver the good news of my admission personally; I felt honoured that he came himself. All their efforts had paid off – finally, my name was on the supplementary list of admitted students in the History department of the Faculty of Arts, University of Etinan.

I smiled and thought, going against the "almighty Dean's" timing to pay and still prevailed to get the admission – that's personal power and the power of money combined. Who doesn't want that?!

"Congratulations, my guy. We will meet again soon," he said, stretching out his hand, which I took in a firm handshake, and thanked him.

By the next morning, lectures timetable was out, and students besieged the school like locust on farmland. Banners of different departments and associations were on display, all with the same message – congratulating the new students and welcoming back the old ones to the campus. Different queues could be seen almost parallel to another. Every day was characterised by these long lines of students, appearing like colonies of ants. Queues for school fees, hostels and recommended Textbooks payments were common features of the early days of resumption. Lawnmowers and manual labourers were helping out in deforestation of the lawn, which had been overgrown with weeds. Everybody seemed to have been dressed to impress; even the lecturers were not left out. The fundamentalist men amongst us had their hairs neatly cut low, while the rather minority conservatives tucked in airtight, fitted shirts, lean ties, and wore eyeglasses with screens like binoculars. Their movements were characterised by an air of importance, seriousness pervaded the university community, and everyone seemed to be behind time, as some had already resumed lectures.

The sidewalk was littered with aged sachets of confectionaries, mostly yoghurts drinks, chocolates and biscuits. The September breeze was warm and soothingly spiced with a fresh fragrance. I remembered each of the classrooms that I entered had finger marks on the heavy dusty desks and chairs. Some corners had cobwebs while the windows sills had lizards' and geckos' faeces competing against each other for decoration. The university stretched into several length of kilometres on a wide landmass. On the northern boundary of the university lay the main campus, which comprised of the administrative block, auditorium, clinic, printing workshop. And behind the VC's office was the Faculty of Science and following in what appeared to be an alphabetical order were other faculties; though not sure of that, but it's easier to think of it in this order. The central car park covered all the available space opposite the faculties.

There was also a long smoothly tarred road that led to the car park; the students had come to name the road "Aluta Avenue". This name and the avenue were synonymous with various students' unrests – the avenue always presented a good ground for such protest marches. It's along this road that great speeches were made by various students' union leaders and activists at different times. A burnt electric power transformer was situated directly facing the central car park. It was on this burnt electric transformer that the students' activist stood and used as their podium to cry injustice, suppression and other unpopular educational policies of the then military government. The institution's fence is an obvious demarcation between the Federal Republic of Nigeria and the Federal Republic of Etinan, as the proud students called the University.

Indeed, as I soon came to discover, the University of Etinan was a Republic within a Republic, which operated with their own drafted constitution. Their president was, and always, a final year student, a product of a well-conducted election, not the type we so often witnessed in Nigeria during every election so far. The office of the President attracted a lot of pecuniary benefits, and it was only eligible to semi-final year students, who would assume office in the next academic season as a final year student; this arrangement ensured that each President stayed in office for no more than one year, making room for others.

The long stretch of the faculty halls and walls served two main purposes, apart from lecture halls for the students: It's where cell meetings of any kind took place and a relaxation spot for the students because of its shade. The other was the big space the walls provided for advertisements. Different posters and bills always found the walls a veritable ground for display. Religious bills took a greater portion of the walls, followed by election posters.

In the religious ones, different fellowships were declaring healings, breakthrough miracles for their expected invitees. The election campaign posters had faces of prominent student activists vying for various elected positions in their departments, faculties and student union government. Some of these aspirants were good looking to behold, while a greater number were defects, a close example of members of the Ape family. Some of these faces had been seen at our lecture halls on their familiarisation visits. I still recalled how these students besieged our classroom and mesmerised us, declaring that they were going to champion the affairs of the students in the next academic session. It was here that my interest in politics and the quest for acceptance, success and power – my primitive drive, was awakened, as I experienced firsthand how all the elected students were treated like heroes; every student held them in high esteem as problem solvers. They were always addressed in respectful slogans, such as Honourabeu (Honourable), Presido (President), great Senator, and articulate Information Minister.

I longed to be like them; they were always so well-dressed. Even at late hours, their tales were always about a series of important meetings they had with the university management bodies, like ASUU, SSANU and NASU. To some extent, they influenced drastic changes in the management and social life of the students within the institution – they were influencers; something I had always wanted. This desire to lead the students motivated me in so many ways. To achieve this newfound passion, I started acting as the self-appointed middleman between my colleagues in the department and our lecturers; even though I was not the class representative. In some occasions, I would be received warmly by the lecturers to my expected desire, and at other times, not so pleasant.

I recall my colleagues and I had some problems with getting the hall we needed for the school's upcoming matriculation ceremony, so, I became the self-appointed speaker and solution provider for our problems. Thus, when I saw Mr. Ojong, a stout, short, middle-aged, lively man, who was part of the matriculation committee, enter into his office, I immediately dashed up to his door before anyone else could get there, knocked and went in without being asked to come in. If I had known that Ojong could be that rude, I would have retreated. He scared the living daylight out of me with a deafening shout, ordering me to get out of his office; I had never felt more humiliated in my life. I ran outside immediately filled with shame. Of course, almost everybody knew that I was the one he had screamed at and called an IDIOT.

So, just to save face, after a few quick steps away from his office, hoping it was far from earshot, I gathered up some courage, forgetting my good manners and respect for elders, and shot back at him, "God punish you; you are an IDIOT too." Even I shocked myself at my own insolence.

That insolent verbal arrow I shot was piercing and loud enough to reach his ears; Mr. Ojong opened the door to come at me, but he only saw me sixty metres sprinting away as fast as I could.

Such was the extent I went in my vain quest to become a student leader; I was already creating and attracting unhealthy attention to myself.

Later that afternoon, the long-awaited details of matriculation were finally announced, and the programme of event was published. Fresh students took the notification with joy after much anticipation and anxiety. In the company of one of my course mates, Bassey, I went to the notice board of the History department to feed my eager eyes. We thronged the place, and soon enough, a sea of human heads was formed. A cacophony of noise disturbed my ears; everybody seemed to be against the institution's choice of venue, which was different from the usual auditorium. The students frowned at the pavilion, which would take only the dignitaries, staff, lecturers and a few students – the best matriculating students, while the rest would be left under the mercy of the hot weather outside. My course mate and friend, Bassey, became interested in the ensuing argument, and immediately, a call for a protest was made, and the students accepted the idea. Shyness or maybe, in this case, timidity, is a weak man's disease and whoever that is afflicted by such should exorcise himself because at the threshold of a just cause this weakness has a way of rearing its ugly head to deflate one. Still recovering from the unhealthy attention that I had attracted to myself less than a week ago, I quietly withdrew with the excuse that I needed to use the toilet. I walked away and stood afar off behind a parked vehicle, while my friend and others protested a just cause.

Shouts of *"we no go gree"* rent the air; some of the returning students taunted us with calls of JAMBITES and JAMBITOS. I stood there frozen with guilt and shame; it would seem I was only good for the bad things and nothing good, so I had to vacate the place and moved a little closer to the crowd but far enough not to be identified as one of them. The students began to march toward the Vice Chancellor's office as was directed by the old students who volunteered. When it appeared that they were making progress, I began to trail them slowly. Moments later, we were at the VC's office entrance, and by just standing there, I was already enthralled by the man with such great intellect that ruled such a big citadel of learning. Anxiety took the better part of me. Students stood there, chanting songs after songs; the majority of the songs were solidarity chants, although most of us ignorantly misconstrued it to be war songs.

A rotund, light-skin, small man came out from the entrance of the VC's office; his face was beaming with smiles, and I wondered what tickled his fancy. The students cheered as soon as the man appeared; I thought that must be the VC. He acknowledged the students' greetings and waved his two short fat hands at the students. Applause from the students greeted the man. In the ensuing cacophony of noises, I heard a great thundering shout with a baritone voice. "G-R-E-A-T N-I-G-E-R-I-A-N S-T-U-D-E-N-T-S!" I stood on my toes to catch a glimpse of the bearer of such a voice; it couldn't possibly be the same small man who had such a big voice, I wondered. Many of us at the rear started jumping high to see; it was the same man! The man spoke for a while, which was meant to be audible and clear enough for our understanding, but I only understood the man's last sentence: "The VC would soon address all of you."

With that, my instinct informed me that the stout man I suspected of being the VC was merely his forerunner. I moved up to the front so that when the VC came out, I would adequately capture his image into my memory. Before I could reach my destination, four well-dressed young men came out and tried to instil some order and quiet, but we kept on with the solidarity chants until a tall man appeared. I was convinced that the tall man standing before us was the institution's Vice-Chancellor, Prof. T. M. Botemi. He was a professor of Physics, one of the first indigenous professors and a graduate of Yorkshire University, London.

I stood there lost in admiration of this distinguished gentleman of wit before me. His hair was thick, full afro with grey intruding into the once-upon-a-time jet-black hair. On the left side of his forehead, he had a canal that looked like an old stitched cut, which ran down to the backside of the head. He had a beard that was about three inches long, and a slimline of black and grey moustache adorned his face. His broad face fits his towering height, and he stood out, sporting a well-ironed transparent white shirt revealing a white singlet under it, over black trousers. A pen and a sheet of paper were in both hands. With this appearance, I concluded that Prof. Botemi was a serious minded-fellow, and a man of great spirit and noble ways. He walked up the pavement with an overwhelming gait; his countenance revealed stress. He first stood akimbo, staring up at the crowd silently as if needing a minute to take it all in, and then crossed both hands behind his back. His guilt-filled expression really lowered his status, in my opinion; perhaps, he is humble by wits. A sacrificial lamb posture was the last thing on my mind going by my impression of the VC; however, I was so struck with this humility that my interest in academics was rejuvenated, especially to become an academic Don like him.

After a few minutes of pinching silence, the VC finally greeted the students. The greeting came almost like a whisper. We responded in like manner, only tinged with fright, thinking our little protest was a misdemeanour. I noticed some of the arrowheads in the protest suddenly became like jellyfish, fidgeting at the sight and sound of the towering man.

Then, as if finding his voice, the VC roared, "Good morning, my young friends."

"Good morning, sir," we all roared in unison.

He smiled and began, having no difficulty with smoothly explaining away the institution's choice of the pavilion against the school auditorium, "I share in your sentiments, but one must take into cognisance in total absoluteness, the ambiguity of inconveniences borne by our distinguished invitees previously."

It was evident that most of us could not

comprehend the VC's grammar. So, there existed neither objection nor question. We assimilated the VC's explanation hook, line and sinker.

Towards the end, we all once again, cowardly responded with a thunderous, "yes, sir" to the erudite Professor's sermon capped with "I hope you understand and agree with me".

Of course, we did not understand and did not agree either, but we dispersed grudgingly into different directions of interest. I had not seen Bassey since the VC came out to address us, so I was walking back alone to the class, then my thoughts went back to the notice board, and I quickened my steps towards that direction. Another student who had stood beside me quiet during the VC's address joined me almost at the same pace; we exchanged greetings and walked together to the History department. He was a few inches taller than me, and he must be the quiet type because, after the exchange of greetings, all efforts by me to drag him out of his quiet shell always met his mute resistance. He must be a good listener, or it might be that nothing about me interested him at the moment. Why am I moving with this dumb fellow? I wondered, frowning. The sentence almost came out of my mouth; his company was simply too boring.

I wondered how people coped with him always mute.

An idea occurred to me, which was to veer off the course we were treading; it was a well-conceived thought, and I instinctively decided to do that. "Alright, Edem," I said, stretching my hand for a departure handshake.

"Where you wan enter?" Edem asked in pidgin.

"Let me see a friend in this department," I said, pointing to the English department.

"Ok now," he said.

"Alright then, later," I responded.

Moments later, I was at the entrance of the English department; I went in and stood at a vantage position, where I could watch the boring master walking like an evil spirit on an errand. His oversize chinos shirt hung on him like an armour. His tight-fitting jean trouser was demeaning; this must be prince poverty himself, a fashion non-starter. When Edem was out of sight, I came out and slowly strolled toward my department.

CHAPTER SIX

It was a fine afternoon in Etinan. The two-day -long non-stop rains had washed every sidewalk and gutter clean, and a tincture of freshness still lingered in the air despite the traffic fumes. The vibrancy of the university town had bounced back the instant the clouds cleared, just in time for the matriculation ceremony coming up in two days. Had the rains continued, it would have been terrible with the muddy ground for most of us new students, who were still going to sit outside under canopies for the ceremony, since the chosen auditorium would not fit everyone.

As I strode through the campus, my footprints were embedded, leaving a piece of me in the wet ground; I loved seeing my prints in the grounds, for some crazy reason it reminded me that I was really a part of this school, but only when the mud was not messing up my borrowed shoes like this. Getting to the faculty of Arts, the halls were crowded with people, and the chaos was so perfect, like a theatre production. There was the couple that was making out on the left side of the hall with no care in the world, and about ten feet farther down, the cliquey babes gossiping. Opposite them, the cliquey guys checking out girls' backsides, and between them, the parade of Theatre Arts students in some funny-looking costumes. On the far end, there were the Fine Art students who never did anything but draw and mold only-God-knows-what, and further away to the right, the Fashion Design students that wheeled mannequins and clothing racks down the halls. Then there was me, not that I fit into any of those groups; I'm a simple History student, who was struggling to meet up with my matriculation demands. I needed to pay for my matriculation gown and other things I would need before the matriculation, which was in two days, and I still hadn't figured out how.

I managed to push past the stream of people to my department. I looked at Etete's watch on my wrist and saw it was almost time for my lecture with

Dr. Uko-Owo – *Introduction to Nigeria History.* The man was something else; some of us were of the view that the lecturer would soon impregnate some of our female colleagues since he was constantly seen in their company in his office. But aside that, Dr Uko-owo was always flowing with solutions for most problems and befriending him could prove helpful. Thus, I thought to check in his office and remind him of the lecture period, but on second thought, I decided differently, and then changed my mind again. Amidst this dilemma, I moved adroitly to his office, and behold, the "Toaster" as students nicknamed him for having canal knowledge of many female students, was coming; the History man was descending the staircase in the company of two female students. Smiling broadly, I gathered courage and reminded him of our lecture after greeting him, and his reply was surprisingly positive. It might be that Toaster recognised my face and remembered those few times I asked and answered questions brilliantly in the class because he responded to my greetings with such warm affection. Yours truly, not quite long after that, Toaster was in the class, everybody scampered to their respective seats, and the business of the hour began.

"Good afternoon, all," he greeted, grinning.

95

We responded cheerfully; I continued grinning like a fool as if my senses had gotten lost in his warmth toward me earlier, and that little friendliness had automatically made us best friends.

"We will continue from where we stopped last week," he said, pausing, "before we start, who can recall what we studied last?"

That was all I needed to wipe the stupid grin off my face and come back to reality.

The question appeared to be a decisive blow as no one made an attempt to answer; at least, it silenced a lot of my colleagues who always showed off. Many of us may have forgotten because the last lecture was the same day and time the matriculation details were released, and we were not quite paying attention as we got distracted by the noise of the other students who had seen it first, and all we wanted to do was to get out and check the notice board, which we eventually all raced out to do.

Three minutes after, still, nobody made an effort to answer the question; no hands were raised among the hundreds in the class. I remember the topic we treated, but my confidence was nowhere to be found. Another bosom friend of mine, Aniedi, also knew the answer to the question, but he was the type that did not like asking or answering questions;

he preferred to remain in his shell or tell another student. He quickly wrote down a few things on paper, adding to the answer of what I already knew we discussed the previous week and suggested that I take up the challenge. I paced up and down, left and right in my mind, took a deep breath, even swallowed saliva, but the courage still eluded me; I sat there mute. By this time, Toaster pointed to a student. The first student he pointed to excused himself on the premise that he was not present on the day the topic was treated. I had this feeling that I would likely be the next person he would ask to answer the question; after all, he knew that I was in the class that day. As a last effort, I raised an unwilling hand into the air, but Toaster ignored my hand. Instead, he pointed to Edidiong, a stammerer who had been out of school for a while. He'd deferred a session because of injuries he suffered in an auto crash, which kept him bedridden for almost a year. Edidiong was the reserved type, but he was not around that day as I recall, and I wondered what he would say.

"Yes; you," Toaster said, pointing at Edidiong and walking towards him.

The whole class was quiet and expectant.

Edidiong wasted no time with his reply, "sir, *I-I-I-I- waaaaas not around; -I-I-I- wen-wen-went to-to attend to-to so-soossss-some medical im-ime-ime-meee-yencies,"* he concluded, looking defiant.

The last word from his sentence had elucidated laughter; unimaginable shame enveloped my whole being, the type that was so thick you could almost touch it; this was my kinsman, murdering the English language. Edidiong had pronounced "emergencies" as *Imeryencies.*

So, Inyang was the next to be picked by Toaster; I guess because he was caught still laughing when every student had kept quiet. There was this confidence in him that made me think he would go into a detailed analysis of the topic. But Toaster sought something different; his area of concern was with the wrongly pronounced word "Emergency". So, he promptly walked toward his right and asked Inyang the correct pronunciation of the word. You see, Inyang was born and brought up in the South-East of Nigeria, but he hailed from my mother's village, Nsit Ekpo. After the death of his father, when he was yet a toddler, his maternal uncle, who was a trader in the South-East, adopted him. Living and growing up there as a young child, Inyang became accustomed to the Igbo language, and the accent was heavily evident in his spoken

English. Thus, doubt of any kind on his inability to pronounce the word was not detected as his comportment was commonplace.

He stood up and adjusted his belt and shirt as if he was facing an opponent in a wrestling contest, and then he picked dirt from his eyes. I wondered if he was not seeing the lecturer clearly; quietness like a graveyard descended on the lecture hall. The whole class was eager and attentive to hear from him. At last, he confidently voiced out, *"The collet plonanshiashom is I-M-A-J-E-N-S-I."*
He was trying to say, "the correct pronunciation is E-MER-GEN-CY"; hence, in making a full sentence, he made matters even worse. We all collapsed into riotous laughter. Even the lecturer could not control his humourous senses as he too, joined in the unexpected comedy which the added full sentence had elicited.

By the end of the lecture, Inyang was nicknamed *Imajensi*. Shouts of Imajensi and more riotous laughter was heard immediately the lecturer concluded the day's lecture and left the class. Inyang tried vainly to dissuade his colleagues from calling him the name, but no, the name had come to stay, because while he was still threatening someone close by, others far away would call the name and take to their heels. Yes, run; you do not want Inyang's thick-veined, muscular, strong hands on you. The scenario continued like that until *Imajensi* became his nickname against his will; nobody called him "Inyang" anymore. Some even changed it to *"Imajen"* to make it stylish. I did try my best though to be more respectful of him and call him his real name, but sometimes, I would mistakenly call him *Imajen*, and then, quickly corrected myself and apologised to him – I believe respect is reciprocal; my grandfather taught me that.

That was my only and last lecture for the day, so I started walking back to my place. Many thoughts invaded my mind as I walked; I slowed my pace as I tried to find answers to the numerous problems plaguing me. First was the matriculation gown, which I have to wear on the matriculation day; a good pair of ready-made black trousers with a long sleeve blue shirt and a matching yellow and black tie. Money was a major player in these needs, and I had exhausted the N50,000 Etete and Terror had given to me; I sent N25,000 to my mother in the village and spent the remaining N25,000 on some payments at school and a few T-shirts. How do I get the money to get these things for matriculation? As for the shoes, I knew Etete would definitely give me any of his father's numerous good ones; it's surprising how he had not questioned me so much about my lack of certain necessities, but rather, provided them without asking for any particular thing in return other than a close friendship. Who does that? I guess he knew I wasn't rich like him; after all, he was the one that came up with the story of me being a rich Doctor's son. Anyway, my perturbed mind kept inventing ideas of making money and destroying it for lack of feasible approach. Money had to be there to cater for the necessary expenses for and on that day.

In all these questions, Etete always surfaced as the only problem solver; thus, my hope was renewed once again since the chief's son would likely rise to the occasion, just as he rose to provide me with accommodation in school, which, of course, came with feeding, and luckily, clothing too – I fit well into his clothes. I shared a self-contained, tastefully furnished apartment with Etete off-campus; the apartment was only a walking distance to and from the campus, although, we sometimes drove to school in Udofia's car or any other rich friend of theirs. Off-campus apartments were the living lifestyle of the big boys in the university, and I had seamlessly fallen into that group by association.

A bit more relieved now, I focused on the frivolous: hordes of students walked past me, and each time this happened, my roving eyeballs scrutinised their clothing. Those students who wore the latest apparels and that closely matched my high-end borrowed ones always got high marks in my mind's score sheet. Insatiable lust was a dangerous asset; it's like an explosive, cool, but when triggered, its effects are outrageous. Suddenly, laughing at myself and shaking my head, I thought – imagine the craziness; despite my all-borrowed lifestyle, I had the audacity to judge other people. And on that note, I picked up my steps and jogged all the way to the apartment. The next day was pretty much the same routine – lectures and back.

Finally, matriculation day dawned postcard perfect. Everything was working in sync for me; I had all I needed to make it an unforgettable day – a designer three-piece black suit, a blue shirt and yellow silk tie, a Salvatore Ferragamo black leather shoes and belt, the matriculation gown, hair neatly cut, and some money in my wallet, all courtesy of Etete as I had envisaged. I arrived the campus at 10:00am looking like I just stepped out of a GQ magazine photoshoot; my own mother wouldn't have recognized me as the son she birthed 19 years ago – I looked like the son of a wealthy medical doctor. The campus was dizzy with activities, everyone running helter-skelter for last-minute things; new students donned academic regalia and proceeded into the formal ceremony of matriculation.

The Academic Matriculation ceremony officially marked the beginning of our academic journey at the University of Etinan, and it's meant to be a big deal. The ceremony brought together the University staff members, students' families and friends, and other important dignitaries to officially welcome and recognize all new students as members of the university community. Thus, every matriculating student was expected to invite their families and well-wishers to bear witness to the school's introduction of the new students and the presentation of the official register in which the new students would sign their names. But while most of the new students had their families present and congratulating them, I had none of my family members present; I neither told my big brother nor my grandpa or mother about the ceremony because I did not want to risk exposing the depth of my family poverty status. I was ashamed of my family. So, I had only my friends in attendance – Etete, Terror, Udofia and their friends that they brought along to support me; they were all looking so good in their well-fitted black suits.

Surprisingly, they did not ask me about the absence of my family at the ceremony. Instead, Udofia complimented my looks, pointing out my expensive designer outfit, which Etete had gifted me as a matriculation gift, and which I also just learnt was a collective gift from three of them. Then Udofia went on to tell me I could always count on them as my family, and so should not hesitate to come to them if I needed anything – *anything at all*. It seemed these friends understood me more than my own family ever did in all my years growing up with them – these people simply loved and accepted me; no questions asked. His kind words almost brought tears to my eyes. But the day was not for crying; it's a day of celebration – my official recognition as a student at the University of Etinan.

Just then, the VC, Prof. T. M. Botemi, was introduced, smiling contentedly, I rose with the other students cheering to welcome him to the podium. He asked us to sit and began his introductory remarks; he is a great orator. After that, the Minister of Education came up to the podium to deliver his speech; it was the longest speech I had ever listened to, but I paid attention and heard most of what he had to say. Most of it was sound advice and inspiring talk that a good parent would give his child, if only our government took their own advice, our country would be a better place for everyone.

Finally, the Provost, Dr. Ekanem Inyang's high-pitched voice rang through the loudspeakers as he mounted the stage, asking all the new students to rise to recite the university's Matriculation Oath, and we began as he signalled, taking the lead.

I hereby promise:
To be a loyal and contributing member of the University of Etinan community;
To abide by the Code of Conduct to assure a responsible environment for learning and living;
To strive for excellence in all that I do;
To respect and nurture my God-given personal dignity and the dignity of others;
To do my best to realise the full potential of my unique personal gifts and abilities;
To lead, serve, and make the world a better place.

I was not sure why, but the last line of the oath captured and held my attention for a while – *"to make the world a better place"*, and I thoughtfully repeated it three more times to myself after the oath reciting had ended. This was the whole essence of education, that out of our learning, we may emerge better persons to make the world a better place for all, I thought. I silently hoped I would be amongst those making the world a better place, not worse like our government people have made it for many of us living below the poverty line.

In addition to the ceremony, the new students were invited to sign the Matriculation book as the university tradition demanded. This signified our commitment to the mission and culture of the University of Etinan. After the Matriculation Ceremony, we continued with our orientation schedules, which included photos, meetings with our academic advisors and orientation leaders, and of course, the evening activities! I took photographs with my friends first as they were in a hurry to leave; then I took some with my course mates, after which I proceeded to meet with our academic advisor. I had no plans for the evening as far as I knew, and Etete didn't say anything about the evening either. Besides, I was too tired and needed to get my sweaty body out of the black suit I was wearing having been seated outside with the sun blazing down on the canopy providing no respite from the heat for hours. So, with nothing else to do, I went back to the apartment to relax for the rest of the day – it was already 5:00pm.

CHAPTER SEVEN

The bang on the door was frighteningly loud. The digital clock on the dresser read 12:05am. In my drowsy state, it was difficult to comprehend who could be knocking on the door at this ungodly hour of the morning. Etete was out most nights till early hours, but he had his own key, so he never knocked whenever he came back. I eventually got up to open the door, but before I could reach for my key, the door was flung open without force; Etete and Terror walked in looking like they were high on something but at the same time appeared calm and coherent. They asked me to relax and sit down, while Etete pulled out three bottles of beer from the fridge, opened them and handed a bottle to each of us. I declined mine, but Terror insisted that I take it, stating that I would need it to help me stay awake and relaxed for the meeting they were there to have with me, so I reluctantly took the bottle and gulped down some.

Then Terror hailed me, "Sequence" laughing mischievously and lifting his hand for a handshake, which I took, laughing but still confused as to what the meeting was about that couldn't wait till morning. And then sudden silence fell in the room, and they both became serious, too serious for comfort. Etete broke the silence, and Terror joined in, both of them taking turns to remind me of the events of my quest for admission into the university at Udofia's place, and how they promised to deliver as long as "I was willing" to cooperate with them, to which I assured them I was "more than" willing. I sat still, wondering where all this history was headed.

"We have delivered; you have admission, and we even added accommodation, feeding, clothing. See how a few hours ago at the matriculation ceremony, you were looking like a GQ model. You're in a sequence, Aniete; it follows an order – I wash your hands, and you wash mine. Now, the time has come for you to deliver on that assurance you gave all of us at Capone's place. It's going down tonight at 1.30am," Terror said.

"Wait. Did you say, "a sequence"? That's what

Udofia called me each time he saw me," I queried.
"Yes; sequence; it's a code for people we like and
want to help change their financial and social
status in life," Etete responded.

I guess all my wondering and gratitude about
how Etete provided my needs without asking for
anything in return was too soon. It finally dawned
on me that the name Udofia had called me from
that fateful day I first met him, "Sequence" meant I
had been placed or I had put myself into a sequence
of events to follow if they got me the help I needed,
which they did without my having to lift a finger.
I didn't even know how or when the fifty thousand
Naira was paid. All I knew was that they'd asked
me to meet and told me that my debt had been
paid and that I had gotten the admission; they even
gave me extra cash to get what I needed to start
school.
"We like you, and we want to change your life for
the best, as you can see, we're already doing that. We
also want to make you more respected and powerful
amongst the students and lecturers; you see how that
lecturer disgraced you that day, shouting and calling
you an idiot; that can never happen to you again.
But you have to join us in our organisation to make
all these and even more available to you. You will not

lack anything you want – money, respect, power, beautiful girls, academic success, anything you want. And you can provide everything that your family needs and help them out of poverty," Terror said.

"You know my family is poor; how?" I asked, surprised.

"We know everything about you; where you live with your elder brother in Etinam; your mother in the village suffering under the wicked hands of your paternal uncles, and even how you used to trek home – your "*legsus*" and pretended about it," Etete answered, smiling.

I was filled with shame, and I covered my face, apologising to them for my pretentious ways, which they simply dismissed as no big deal.

"Also, Ani, we keep the organisation a secret from outsiders; it's only for a select few, and we want to upgrade your status to be part of that select few. It starts from now; we've come to get you for your induction into the organisation; the ceremony starts at 1.30am – less than 40 minutes from now. Udofia is the head of the organisation - the Capone, and that's why he called you Sequence; he chose you, to change your life," Etete concluded.

Of course, at the mention of "secret" it finally registered – this was one of the secret cults in school! But at this point, I was already backed up against the wall; I was in a twisted situation, and there was no untangling myself from this twist. Looking into their eyes, I could only see two options – go willingly or go forcefully with them. And the force could end up with me maimed or dead. I chose the immediate, more comfortable option.

You see, one thing that always struck me about these secret cults was that no matter how dark they seemed, there was always a nugget of hope that drew people in; they came offering desperate, confused people a path towards something positive and then twist the way so gradually that the members miss the turn, but not so much that new members wouldn't get attracted to join them. These guys had offered more than enough attraction and effortlessly lured me too deep inside to escape when this moment to give back finally came; thus, it goes without saying, I gave in to their request. I was already in the sequence, and I couldn't break out of it.

However, I must confess that as much as it felt like I had no better option, all the gains that Terror laid out for me sounded like beautiful music in my ears, fueling my primitive drive and pulling me deeper so that all resistance and sense of alarm dissolved away, and the lust for all of it took precedence. I hurriedly got dressed and followed them out the door.

The induction or initiation ceremony had no particular formalities; a sizeable number was enough to start, and songs preluded it. Both old and new members joyously danced around a fire made up of used vehicle tyres. The merry throng went wild with jubilation each time a new song was introduced. Mixed alcoholic liquor was freely poured out to everyone, and it was compulsory to finish your drink. Pouring it away could attract the wrath of the Capone, Udofia. After a while, a few more students joined us. Many of these faces I saw were strange to me. Quickly, they fell in line with the rest of us, increasing the tempo and projecting the songs led by the Chief Sailor.

The Chief Sailor is the member with the amour of songs of the organisation in his kitty. His office always had aides that are called 'Songitos', whom he often delegated work to in the event he was indisposed. The Songito that would prove himself most worthy and capable eventually rose to become the Chief Sailor; he assumed the position on the graduation or demise of the sitting Chief Sailor and led the songs during every initiation ceremony.

After almost an hour of singing and dancing, the Chief Sailor signalled the end of the songs in a typical choir fashion, and silence settled in our midst. He turned to face the new members and with hands raised, he said, "Welcome to the Black Scorpion organisation; you have done yourself a great service to be here tonight for this special occasion to initiate our new Scorplings," he paused as everyone cheered before continuing, "it is now time for us to get to know each other."

So, that's the name of the cult, Black Scorpion, and I was considered a Scorpling – that wouldn't be for long as I was no baby; I thought.

The introduction of both old and new members began with the Chief Sailor –Tekena Peters, Engineering, 300 level, and his alias, Chief Sailor. The second person to introduce himself was a tall slim youth, a Songito – Ini Udoh, Mathematics, 200 level; he had the best voice, so much better than the Chief Sailor's, and his complexion seemed a little fairer than normal. After several introductions, the stage was set for my introduction, which I did in style. I began with my name, age, department, level, and ended it with my Capone-given name - Sequence. This received great applause. The Chief

Sailor interrupted the mood by commending my style and boldness so far in their midst, saying that I may attain an intimidating profile soon enough if I maintained this tempo to becoming a grandmaster. The process continued until seventy-nine stood the last number and person. Then, we followed the instruction of the Chief Sailor to place our right hand on our chest to recite the pledge of the organisation after him, and then the objectives were made known to us by other senior fellows in the system.

The thirty-seven new members were taken aside for another drilling for what was termed as "assimilations". We were stripped naked, blindfolded and ordered to search for the armoury box deposited somewhere in the bush. I already knew that the initiation ground shared the same boundary with the cemetery and had a definite demarcation of a brickwall fence. This exercise took us almost two hours, tending towards 3.15am, I presume. At a point, all the noise died down, except the barking phantom of the cemetery. Amidst this, we were thoroughly beaten and punched whenever the opportunity presented itself. Despite this inhuman treatment, none of us cried or begged for mercy; we were simply not allowed that luxury and Undertaker ensured that. Since I had been hanging out and enjoying the company of some of them at different places and times before tonight, I guess the familiarity placed me at an advantage to get through the excruciating exercise, as I believed that whatever they did to me here was not for evil but for my good because they cared for me as a friend already; yes, I made myself believe that. And at our casual hangouts, I was often called into a tête-à-tête with Etete and Zonal Butcher – Undertaker, Boma Seriake; although then I didn't know he was the Black Scorpion's Undertaker.

There was something about Boma or Bomb as he's fondly called, that drew people to him. No doubt, he was good looking – 6.3ft tall, slim, with well-defined bone structure and fine muscle build; his voice was husky with a hint of seductive drawl to it, and every step he took was in slow motion compared to almost anyone else I know, but it was more than all that. He was quiet, but not out of shyness; it was a reservedness, like a conscious choice to observe the lay of the land before he got in. He wasn't snobbish; he was friendly and welcoming in body language, but I never saw him go out and deliberately make a friend, they just came to him. Nothing was threatening about him, yet he was the "threat to life" himself, and he had zero tolerance for any show of emotions or weakness. There was something about him that revealed he was from a good home and well-brought-up, but maybe, like me, his primitive drive had been touched, or he was simply "Lucifer Devil" personified – sleek, smooth, seductive and pure, undiluted evil to the human race.

As the activities of the early hours continued, Capone with the aid of other senior members set up bonfire into a burning heap, and machete and various other weapons were brought out from the armoury box that one of us found in the cemetery during the assimilation process, a total of sixteen guns – two revolvers, five AK 47 and nine M19. A flashlight was pointed at the wooden box, turning to see the bearer, I beheld Capone, a familiar, yet unfamiliar fellow – Udofia. Throughout the night, he was different and unrecognisable to me; he was stern and grinding his teeth seemed to have suddenly become his favourite past time.

Looking straight at me, he commanded in a hoarse voice, "Open the second box and bring out its contents."

I obeyed with a passion as if I enjoyed the errand, but it was really because Capone was greatly feared and dreaded; I dared not take knowing him before this night for granted. Besides, gladly obeying him was an avenue for me to rub shoulders with him at this new, different level. Shiny brownish metal clinked against each other in a heap, and just like I was instructed, I dipped my ten fingers into the box and cupped them in my hands. I needed not to be educated on the names and usage of the items – these were BULLETS!

At this time, the bonfire was now blazing; the tongue would spread intermittently as if attempting to consume us all. A circle was formed around the fire. The Capone brought out two bottles of alcoholic liquor and a drinking glass in the other hand. Two members, Etete and Unyime, followed him immediately; he instructed all of us to be brave like the Spartan and bear pains without betraying our feelings.

"Everybody's blood will be collected for the next stage of our programme," he announced loudly and continued, "this information is for only the new members of this noble organisation. May your blood clot if you disappoint yourself."

With this announcement, old members filed out of the circle, leaving us. This stage of the initiation got most of us jittery as our blood would be collected, and none of us had an idea on the manner it would take. I thought it was going to be through a syringe, which I whispered to another new member beside me. Low-tone murmuring was gaining altitude by this time.

"S-I-L-E-N-C-E," Capone barked, "this is not a market or a gathering of Jew-men, be warned; it is a longer way to Golgotha from here." As silence befell us, Capone's eyes did not lose its stoniness, nor his voice the tinge of evil.

"Whoever that is not man enough should fall-out for the business of the day to begin," he commanded in a harsh, husky voice that had become strange to me. Our eyes were looking for the effeminate among us. Capone's eyeballs were blazing wickedly, and his eyes were shining like Nigerian policemen's flashlight until they settled on me. He peered down at me suspiciously, then as if satisfied, he gave the order, "Collect their blood."

The first donor, Udeme, stretched forth his right arm and in a quick moment, Unyime tapped the tip of the sharp knife on his palm, and the donor cried out in pain. Immediately, Etete sent a horsewhip lashing down hard on his bareback. This left me shell-shocked; who would have thought that the same soft-spoken, kind Etete that I live and eat with every day was capable of such inhumanity. Etete, like Terror, was a Hitman, but Terror was the organisation's Roaming Sniper. Hitmen were members whose assigned tasks, more often than not, resulted in the death of their victims. The promotion of a hitman in the organisation was often rapid, especially when armed with a track-record of several successful hits within a given timeframe. A Roaming Sniper was a hitman who discharged his skirmishes in another institution successfully. He was always rewarded financially, and sometimes, the female cult members are instructed to satisfy them sexually, or non-member female students are threatened or kidnapped and forced to "willingly" do this without making it appear like rape – she must appear to enjoy it as much as he does, or suffer worse fate. Suffice to say, nobody got to the higher positions of authority on a platter without being an avid killer. These were the challenges before me, and also, every new member present to remain relevant in the organisation.

Anyway, the whip quieted down Udeme. His hand was turned such that his blood easily dripped into a waiting cup. He slightly winced in pain, shaking his head occasionally. For those of us who were to follow, we died many times before our turn. Goose pimples were all over my body. Three other donors followed after Udeme, and indeed they were Spartans; none of them uttered a sound throughout the period. It was now the turn of the fifth student, Ukpong, History, 100 level; my course mate. He turned and looked at the rest of us; he must have wished the knife and the cup to pass over him. Out of great fright, he surrendered.

"Please, I'll not be able to do it," he murmured, panting like a fish just out of water.

His statement had jolted everybody; I heaved and breathed out, expecting the unexpected. Ukpong was told to lie on his stomach and cover his cowardly face.

Unyime walked to me; it was finally my turn. I presented my hands like a Spartan, but when he raised the knife to slit my head, fright forced me to tilt my head backwards, dodging the stab. The move helped a little but almost worsened the situation because the knife cut me around my eyebrow, just a little above my left eye, missing my eye by less than a quarter of an inch. Blood gushed out and spilt into my eye. I didn't understand why my head was chosen for the cut, instead of my hand like the others. Thus, I narrowed it down to the proverbial saying, *whom much is given, much is expected.* These people had given me much. The injury was deep and painful, but I had no choice than to endure it like a Spartan to avoid being flogged with a horsewhip by Etete, my own dear friend and housemate.

After this, Ukpong was ordered to roll on the ground – one end to the other, before us that completed the blood donation. By this time, Capone had started threatening him that he would not leave the place alive except he cooperated with us by donating his own blood. More beating was unleashed on Ukpong, and he screamed as loud as his lungs could take, though we're not supposed to be heard in the thick forest. Thus, he was continuously beaten to quietness. This effeminate attitude of Ukpong infuriated the Bossman, Etim Nkanta, the second in command to the Capone, who had been quiet since while awaiting his part of the initiation event and trying to control himself under the influence of God-knows-what drugs. He made a sign, which was understood by Capone; I guess that was to grant him permission as Capone's right-hand man to step out of his quiet zone. He rose to his full-bodied, 5.11ft height, taking off his hood as he raised his head, revealing a face filled with anger and eyes blazing red with the fire of hatred; nonetheless, a handsome, boyish face. He was a great Mixologist; he knew what drinks and powders or tablets to mix to get a certain desired result.

He instructed Unyime to pour some Gin into the glass of blood collected from us, and then add some tablets, which he'd handed him, to the mixture. While this was going on, a human skull was repeatedly tossed into the air and caught by Bossman. After a while, we were given the mixture in the glass to drink. A gin bottle cover was used to measure the mixed liquor for all of us new fellows. We drank and became *Useme* – like zombies in the process. One after the other, we swore using the human skull to an oath of allegiance to the organisation. No feeling or compassion was left in us, the dreadful fear of death was suddenly gone, and nothing mattered to us anymore in the world. I felt like punching the President of our country and demanding an explanation on the incessant industrial action of the University's academic staff. It later dawned on me that those tablets I saw being mixed along with the blood and gin were mind-changing drugs. I felt somewhat dizzy as if hypnotised. Ukpong was still rolling on the ground, and Bossman called out to him, giving him another opportunity to perform the ritual or face the consequence of his refusal. But he still declined. In a flash, when we were not observing, Ukpong took to his heel into the dark, running as fast as his short legs could carry him. The Capone ordered us to chase him and bring him back dead or alive, or else we would take his punishment. Like leopard after its prey, we charged after him, and a few minutes later, I was in the lead closing in on Ukpong; I pounced on him immediately he was within my reach, and we both fell to the thorny ground. Others surrounded us, and the coward was captured.

Bossman, Etim, appeared and instructed us to do away with him to avoid the possibility of our secret being leaked. We beat, kicked, and punched him on every available part and space of his body; he groaned and shouted for help. At a point, no sound was heard from him anymore. Then, we dragged him to our spot as a present to our Capone for our bravery. Everybody seemed to be satisfied that he was not allowed to escape. The Chief Sailor, Tekena, released a triumphant song, to which we all danced around Ukpong. Although Capone commended us, he was also quick to remind us of the consequences if we had allowed Ukpong to escape.

"We would not be fooled," he thundered, "now let him go the way of the coward that he is."

The Capone made a sign, and Undertaker, Boma stepped forward with a knife and two shovels. And with the swiftness of a skilled workman, he sliced open Ukpong's throat; I guess to ensure he was more dead than death – that was the only reason I could think of. He handed the two shovels to two old junior members, and quickly, they dug a shallow grave, and Ukpong's body was dragged into it. Then Undertaker gave one of the new converts a pistol and ordered him to shoot the "overly dead" boy again and again until his face was unrecognisable, which he did, and another two were commanded to cover him with the earth. I peeped at him and saw that one of the shots had penetrated his skull from the forehead while the other shots were on his eyes, cheeks and chest; he was unrecognisable indeed. We hurriedly gathered our tools into the bags and boxes and assembled before Capone and Bossman for the roll call. A circle was formed as we numbered ourselves. The total number stood at seventy-eight.

"At least, nobody escaped," the Capone said with

an air of satisfaction. "The Black Scorpion initiation rite has come to an end. Everybody is on his own from now till later," he looked frantically like a rat fleeing from danger.

"If you are caught, do not disclose any information about this organisation, and we, on our part, will do everything possible to get you out. That's a promise we do not take lightly."

Then Bossman stepped forward and announced, "we are not going in a group but separately and in different directions," he paused, "and until the vultures see a need to gather, we'll meet again soon," he said, putting on his hood again and walked away.

Everybody started moving. Two of Capone's bodyguards followed him. Others moved in different directions as Capone instructed. I looked back at the spot we buried Ukpong, and I knew for sure that no eyes would see his eyes ever again – a 100 level, History student, who came into the university full of dreams and his whole life ahead of him, now cut short just like that – we, I, had just killed a human being. That day something in me died and got buried along with Ukpong.

****

It's been three weeks since my initiation into the cult, and within that short period, we had carried out all kinds of attacks against rival cult group members. Last night was one of such attacks, and we killed two students in the crossfire. We needed to lay low for a while, till the dust settled, so every evening we hung out in our hide-out smoking *Ikong-ekpo* as if our violent lives depended on it. Acrid stench from the smoke trailed around us like fumes from a locomotive engine. Occasionally, sparks from the smoke stick would drop, and we would scamper into safety to avoid it landing on our clothes, laughing at each other. Although none of us was in a smoking competition with the other, we were constantly inhaling the smoke deeply with an accustomed hypnotised feeling. Being the one that was put in charge of our smoking adventure always sped adrenalin in my metabolism; I get to order and pay for the *Weed* and whatever else we wanted to smoke, so, I was always given more than enough money because excuses for lack of smoke were not tolerated, and so far, I had not disappointed, which earned me more respect in the group. I was poor but fierce. Thus, over a period of three short weeks, I had developed too much confidence, even when without Etete's Beretta M9 pistol, which was fast becoming mine.

Capone had called for a meeting, so all four of us were headed to the Black Scorpion secret place. I could hear our footsteps marching dry leaves beneath us, and since all my three counterparts, Undertaker, Terror and Etete, were armed to the teeth, I walked dizzily in the front, enjoying their protection, if I didn't know better, I would think I was their leader, and they were my bodyguards. As I staggered on, I looked up into the horizon, the moon announced its presence and seemed to be accusing me of something as it stood eerily trained on me in the warm breezy evening; I could almost swear I saw my dead father's face on that moon – I must be very high. I looked away quickly. Under the trees, wild insects flew after each other, savouring the warm breeze, one came at me, and I instinctively swiped it off with my hand as we veered off the road into the familiar bush, dodging and jumping over wild shrubs. A short distance ahead of us, we heard the familiar, cheering voices of comrades in our system; it felt like returning home from a successful war.

CHAPTER EIGHT

I laid wide awake in bed, restless, and mostly staring up at the ceiling after several fruitless efforts to sleep. Many thoughts swam through my river of imagination, fighting for recognition. The most outstanding was the unemployment rates in the country. From available facts given to us at a seminar some days ago by a seasoned Economist on the topic: *"Curbing the Unemployment Rates – the Menace and the Consequence"*, the erudite Professor of Economics had expressed the consequences for the country if nothing was done to arrest the unfortunate situation. According to his well-researched statistics, he said that a total of about two hundred and seventy thousand fresh graduates were being produced yearly from eighty-one tertiary institutions. With an alarming decay in the university system, the majority of these graduates were half-baked, and therefore, lacking in the required skills needed by various organisations in the country. The man of intellect had warned and enumerated many vices that would engage this army of applicants, like armed robberies, drug trafficking, kidnapping, assassins, fraud, political thuggery for the male, while the female graduates would elevate prostitution to a higher level. Another problem, also, was the prevailing poor infrastructure on ground.

These staggering facts pummelled my troubled soul. Over-crowded lecture halls that would shame Guantanamo Bay prison, and the poor facilities we had to contend with at school troubled me the most. Morally bankrupt lecturers, who allocate marks to the highest bidder and female students that were willing to unlock their reserved private areas. I kept wondering the kind of future the Nigerian youth was being groomed to face. Recycled, outdated reading materials called "Hand-Outs" had come to replace our textbooks just to satisfy the lecturers' greed for financial gain. Research of any kind had been dumped in the cesspit of many institutions. Imagine! Teaching students Economics that is all about assumptions, but after the real cost. What an irony! The eighteenth-century banking system in the millennium; accounting principles that aid fraud instead of uncovering it! My mind working in a dizzying frenzy delved into the Faculty of Agriculture; it was surprising that the Egyptian irrigation system of the Mosaic and renaissance period was what the students were still being taught. With an estimated fourteen to twenty children per family, how do you feed this overpopulated country which encourages polygamous marriages?

My thoughts journeyed down to the secondary schools – a critical stage for qualitative graduate education, and I was shocked to the marrow at my realisation of what is left of the system. Since the take-over of post-primary school education from the missionaries, the eventual collapse of the system became inevitable. Secondary schools were now being managed on the whims and caprices of the principals. Then came the private schools to the rescue; everything became private. No repeating of class for the teeming *"mumu"* population – pass or fail, everyone got promoted; I guess that's their idea of the mantra, "no child left behind". Parent cashed on it and with the collaboration of the schools' proprietors, "special centres" for all examinations started, and every *"dollapo"* made an "A" in all examinations, be it WAEC, GCE, NECO, JAMB, etc. Discipline was gradually given freedom from the schools; students who hitherto respected and feared their tutors were now exchanging fisticuffs with them at the slightest provocation. There were no more quiz competitions; school debates had been buried. And what was speedily gaining prominence were school parties, while looking forward to reality television shows.

Furthermore, there was this so-called Nomadic education being practised in the northern parts of the country. Despite the outcry that greeted the implementation of this policy regarded as a conduit pipe to siphon public funds, it was allowed to stay. Till date, nobody has deemed it fit to evaluate the funds so far expended on the scheme. This left room for questions: Where are the graduates of the Nomadic education? Where are the Nomadic teachers produced over the years? In one of the documented bulletins supporting this form of education, I saw one of the children of cattle rearers sucking raw milk from the tits of the cow. I was disgusted by the picture, which made me ask: Was the little boy thirsty for water or was he in a routine pleasure? The medical profession had severally cautioned parents on feeding their wards with cow milk to avoid children developing cow brains. In this scenario, should education still follow them or the other way around?

While still trying to make sense of the nomadic education, my attention got snatched away by the state of our sporting system and its facilities. This latest examination stemmed from the fact that Etete and I recently drove past the State Stadium and saw the rot; it was in a deep, embarrassing mess. The swimming pool had become a typical man-made-pond in full view – algae, spirogyras, bacteria, weeds, frogs and insects had taken over the Olympic-size pool and found it a favourable breeding ground. Once the glory of the State, the stadium now a shadow of itself, completely lacking any kind of care and maintenance. The racetracks, which in time past could boast of professional athletes, sweating it out on the track for the country's glory and honour, was completely covered by grass.

All of these realities grated badly on my nerves; I wanted to punish everyone responsible for these decays. I wanted to make a difference, bring about change, and as a far as I knew, it seemed the only language this powers-that-be understood was violence. When the people of a nation suffer so much deprivation and violence from the authorities that should protect and serve them good, then the violent amongst the people must apply the same force to serve them justice. Coming to this conclusion, my eyes finally began to feel sleep beckoning, and just then, there was a knock on the door. I sat up and reached for my pistol under the mattress, and since the door was unlocked, I spoke out loud, asking the fellow to come in without bothering to ask who it was.

It was Nsa, the Black Scorpion's new *"informinua"* – he delivered messages to the members about upcoming meetings and operations, and also acquired crucial information for the group to keep us steps ahead of our enemies; I consider him our own in-house FBI agent, and he's very good at his job. Seeing how he was sweating all over, I suspected that something was wrong. I got up and offered him a seat on the bed. He declined. He was only interested in delivering the message; I believed he had many other contacts to meet up.

"Assignment dey...ooo," he said in pidgin English, "these SU (Scripture Union) people are all out on us; they are embarking on a 'great march' as they tagged it," he said as his chin quivered slightly.

"They will start from the Theater Arts department towards the Lawn Tennis Court to stop our gathering tonight. So, Capone has ordered all of us to assemble one hour earlier than expected to confront these fanatics at 10:30pm at the same venue. So, load yourself…o," he concluded.

He barely finished the last sentence when he hurriedly rushed out of the room; I followed to see him off, but his pace was faster than mine, so, I bade him farewell till the appointed time.

At the appointed time, we assembled at the pre-arranged venue. Fully armed to the teeth, Bossman dished out precise instructions in low tones, and the message was clear. We split up into two groups and camped at different vantage points to avoid being detected and to regroup seamlessly at the appointed venue of the assignment. By this time, members of the Scripture Union had started marching towards our area. Swiftly, we moved to the Lawn tennis court where the SU had targeted to spend some time praying to destabilise the "forces of darkness" as we were termed. We were strategic, and all our arms were out and set to make our move against them. On instruction from Capone, we formed two lines, each facing the opposite direction.

In the faraway distance from the main campus area, we could hear songs of praise rendered by the SU on their way, towards the male hostels. Everybody became alert, all belts were tightened, and head scarfs were decked. Those of us with guns confirmed our readiness with signals. The Bossman commanded us to squat, which we obeyed quickly. We knelt with one leg pointing our arms at the approaching SU members. It appeared that they had suspected our presence because about a hundred metres away, their praise chant changed. They bound and hurled curses at every known name of hierarchy in our organisation. The name CAPONE was very prominent on their lips; it was rebuked at every opportunity. I could see Udofia, our Capone adjusting himself each time the name was rebuked. He got infuriated and barked down orders at the invading SU members. This met a quick response from their leaders, binding and cursing even more, while the members praised and cheered.

"I'd spare your lives by giving you time to vacate this area now," Capone yelled at them.
"We would grant your wish if you would accept Christ and follow us," the SU leader replied.
"Be warned; you guys are invading someone's

territory without cause," Capone threatened.

"Be informed as well that we're not of the world," the leader retorted boldly.

"Then go to your world; you hypocrites."

"We came in peace for you to repent," their leader yelled back.

"Then you would go in pieces and regret if you don't leave here now," Capone warned.

"Touch not the Lord's anointed and do my prophets no harm," he responded, quoting from the Holy Scriptures.

"I'm happy you were not told to confront us," answered Capone.

While this was going on, the SU members were constantly cheering their leader's bravery each time he replied, daring Capone.

"Look; you guys have to retreat this very moment," Capone said, more impatient than ever.

"Lord, change their hearts and evil ways," the leader prayed, stretching his hands up to the sky.

This statement infuriated Bossman, and he crept to the spot where Capone was hiding, whispered something to him, and crept back to us.

"You have one minute to leave this place and go to heaven; otherwise you guys will see hell on earth today," Capone barked.

"The Israelites have always conquered their

enemies –,"

"One!" Shouted Capone, cutting him off.

"So, who are you uncircumcised Philistines," the leader continued.

"Two!" Capone continued counting.

"We come against you in the mighty name of JES –,"

"A-T-T-A-C-K!" Capone roared at us on top of his voice before the SU leader could complete the name.

I guess he was too livid such that he could not hold himself to count up to sixty to give them even one minute. But he was meticulously pedantic; perhaps throughout history, there was no humane war, since guns were always part of the arsenal. We were constraint to speak the language they would understand, for guns spoke only one language. Thus, we surged at them like rampaging leopards, and it was such a great delight to see these "Godly brethren" fleeing like antelopes.

"Shoot into the sky but not at them," Bossman instructed as we were closing in on them.

The ones amongst us with guns fired into the sky, and I marvelled as the seemingly powerful binders and cursers fled into different directions like sheep without a shepherd. Some of the coward brothers and sisters capitulated at the first gunshot. They knelt, raising their hands into the air. I followed a group that veered into another direction, and some of my men trailed behind me. We captured a handful, mostly females and dragged them back to the tennis court.

Sharp cries of agony from the fleeing brethren were heard not too far away; many among them called unto their Creator. My group captured nine female students and two males, while another group returned with five males and thirteen females. Apparently, Bossman was not interested in the males, so he personally stabbed them with his machete and allowed them to run away.

With his flashlight, he selected two of the females considered extremely beautiful in the darkness – one for himself and one for Capone; their clothes were torn apart, revealing their underwear. Some of our guys kept surveillance for any intruder, while others took turns satisfying themselves sexually with the rest of the girls according to seniority in the system. Poor girls; their pleading fell on deaf ears as they were unmercifully pounded. Capone and Bossman penetrated their catch carefully as if it were consensual and on the softness of a mattress with fine linen in the bedroom. To us, it was woe to the vanquished. And some of us, who hitherto could not utter a word to ask a girl out, were now bold enough under this circumstance, in pitch darkness, to use commanding words, thrusting hard on top of their conquered victims. Everybody had one thing to do with the unfortunate girls; the silent rule in the organisation was that everyone had to be seen doing something to the girls – we all had to take turns to mete out our own punishment to our captives. Thus, some of us inserted our fingers into the girls' battered valleys. Even lily-livered Nsa, our Informinua, was fumbling with two round mounds on the chest of one of the girls. But a good number of our guys outrightly raped the girls, and the unlucky ones amongst them had three to four guys taking turns with them, especially if such a girl had vital assets. It was there that I realised that beauty itself, although abstract, had its own pitfall.

There was this short SU female student amongst them with pitiful, scary face that disinterested all of us. She was what can be called a good example of *"woh-woh"* – ugly babe. With her terrible natural Afro hairdo and mammary glands that grew out of proportion; she wore a long-pleated skirt over her extra-large buttocks. She was not worth anything except a domestic servant in a rural village. Behold, "Miss Ugly", if there was any pageant like that. I wondered how she got admitted with all the negative vicissitudes adopted to accommodate her and her "assets" as if beauty was now a criterion for university admission. Nobody would touch her, even with a long pole; thus, we banished her to her fate by forcing her to lie face down at a distance throughout the duration the episodes lasted.

There were groans among our victims; many regretted the moves they adopted and constantly begged to be set free with promises never to confront us. Some of the female victims, in the peak of anguish, called the many names of the host of heaven. Pity and guilt invaded my mind, but I was helpless as such feelings could be termed weak, and I knew the penalty for weakness. The SU members that I saw were helpless students who were led blindly into an unnecessary assault on their person by their leaders' ego. I could boldly sum up that they were not solid Christians, but frail-faith fanatics on a suicide mission. When defenceless students, in the dead of night, march up against a formidable foe, who derived pleasure in inflicting pains to others, much is left to be desired. To me, they were just a panicky mob, not a fighting force – whether physical or spiritual; they never stood a chance. We were flesh and blood with physical weapons, and they came physically at us refusing to acknowledge that to their own peril. Even the Holy book puts it aptly, *"the weapons of our warfare are not carnal but spiritual through God for the pulling down of strongholds…"* – the SU leaders had it all twisted with their emphasis on *spiritual forces* in high places. We were physical forces they could see on ground with both eyes open. I felt sad for their ignorance because they didn't have to go through this terrible ordeal; they could have stayed in their rooms or place of worship to pray, and who knows, maybe successfully pulled down the strongholds they believe was holding the rest of us bound. How do you face a man with a gun, telling him you bind him? Even David in the same Holy Book knew to take Catapult and good stone with him to face Goliath. I must say their woes were self-inflicted, and I still can't decipher the motives behind their bare-faced boldness. *Chai!* Ignorance indeed destroys a people.

When we were satisfied, our captives were set free

on Capone's instruction. I thought they would race off to a safe distance, but I was wrong, about four of the girls could barely get on their feet. I assisted one of them whom I had done something with to get on her feet; she sobbed all through the exercise. Most of them walked with difficulties, and at a point, one had to crawl like a crab, while others strolled as if their legs were cramped. Tears of regret welled up my eyes, which I quickly stopped from rolling down my cheeks before anyone could notice. The girls were all moving like rejected widows on their way to perdition. As they kept going, led by the woh-woh girl, we gathered quickly and numbered ourselves in the lowest possible tones but still audible enough to hear each other, and then our signature Black Scorpion departure commenced – leaving in different directions. Morbid fear engulfed my soul; I knew I had taken the wrong course. That moment, I remembered that I was a Church boy some years back. Now, I was among the legion of demons parading the campus and terrorising the institution at night. Since my abode was not far away, it did not take me long to reach the apartment I shared with Etete. Under the foot mat, I picked the keys and vanished inside the room, took some strong sleeping pills, and in a matter of minutes,

I fell into a troubled sleep.

I was woken by a knock on the door. Immediately, I became frost with fear, and like a burglar on a routine assignment, I tiptoed to the door and peeped through the keyhole. Behold, it was a familiar foe, Terror. He entered, beaming with mischievous smiles embedded with a tinge of envy. He had been ill for a while, and therefore, could not participate in the assignment last night; it was obvious he came to hear our exploits directly from the horses' mouth. *"Mehn...* the talk is everywhere...o; *you guys don create effect...o,"* he said displaying a weak smile.

"My guy; I don tire," I said, trying to change the topic of discussion that he was introducing, "I just need some sleep."

"Comot there; who you wan deceive, abi you think say I be mumu? You guys been get enough babes to chop for free, make I tell you," he said, waving me away with the back of his hand, *"Chai,* how I wish I was there," he sighed, snapping his fingers in regret, "these fucking sickness is fucking me up."

I pointed at the half bottle of Brandy given to me by Etete, which was in a corner under the desk, but he refused.

"By next week, I go dey ok. No be you go give me shack, but na me and you go shack together tire."

While he was still talking and counting his losses, I dozed off again until the heat of the sun started having its effect on me, as usual, there was no power to run the air conditioner. I woke to meet an empty room; Terror must have gone some hours ago, leaving the door ajar.

From outside the veranda, I could hear enough to know that last night's incident was a major topic dominating the neighbourhood; I played deaf to most of the inviting scenarios. Sometimes, I felt so tempted to butt in and analyse the event whenever falsehood was introduced, but I always restrained myself not to get carried away. No group claimed responsibility, and one of our rivals were constantly mentioned. Many people condemned the acts in strong terms. The fiercest of the criticism was from the Dean of Students Affairs; his short speech was aired in the university's Radio Station, and also the national news stations at night.

He was in his usual French suit saying, "this barbaric act of these monsters in our midst must be condemned in no uncertain terms, and for those unfortunate victims, my heart goes out to you."

This edited part of the speech went on for three days. The university decided to foot the hospital bills of the victims.

This event led to the clamp-down on all our activities on campus. Routine stop and search were conducted in classrooms, lecture halls and hostels. Those of us who were off-campus students were off the hook. However, many of us were placed on the watch list. Fortunately, my name did not feature anywhere. While in a queue entering the Access Control outlet through the pedestrian entrance on campus, students would be frisked before and behind me, but I would only be parted on the back and asked to go on my merry way. This was due to my carefully concealed display of innocent looks. Information also had it that some highly privileged individuals' children were among our victims – this gladdened my heart; I saw it as a kind of payback in full measures. Though they were pulling all the strings to find the culprits who meted out this violent act on their children, I wasn't troubled by that. After all, their wards had benefited from their looting of government treasury and made their living out of my own misery, yet I am a Nigerian.

I slept throughout the day and woke in the evening, ate some food, and then tackled some class assignment before going back to bed.

CHAPTER NINE

The passage of the light slowed, and the sounds became as if underwater. Aside from the pounding of my heart, no muscle would move. The pounding struck a rhythm to the words of his execution, as the cold, black steel became Ekpedeme's judge and jury. The bullet entered as if he was nothing, just meat, blood and bones, blasting a cavity in his chest as it burst crimson into the cloudy late afternoon. His face, so friendly in life was frozen, eyes open, mouth slack, as he was propelled backwards. His eyes held mine, pleading, and in those fractions of seconds, he was there, and then he was gone; the dreams in his eyes that had been his future simply vanished.

I woke with a start, sweating profusely; it was yet another nightmare. Rubbing my head, I got up and poured myself a shot of Vodka, swallowing the liquid in one gulp and poured another to drown the feeling of guilt and fear gnawing at me.

The horror associated with the brutal killings we had perpetrated continued to haunt me for several days now. And now, more than ever before, I became more determined to frustrate any other moves to dispatch threat letters to our rivals or would-be victims. Many times, I tried, and many times, I failed. But since there was no harm in trying, I persisted. After all, the monkey only learns to jump from tree to tree after each fall. On two occasions, I succeeded in thwarting my organisation's effort; these acts also wove suspicion around me until Etete intervened. When this happened, Nsa was appointed, in the interim, as the only dispatch man for the threat letters, added to his duties as the Informinua, even though the delivery of threat letters was above his pay grade – he was not a hitman. But I was not perturbed as long as being a forerunner to death was not part of my job description.

Though I did not pull the trigger that killed Ekpedeme, I might as well have been his executioner; I was part of the meeting where the plan to execute him was hatched, albeit reluctantly, and I did nothing to stop it. His death was the most painful of all the killings. Not that the others' death was not special or that families and loved ones did not value their lives, but in hindsight, I had attached a kind of emotion to the person involved. Ekpedeme was a fiery critic, a pain in the neck of the school authority. As one of the students crying ALUTA on the campus, he had stepped on too many toes – worst of all, the evil toes of the Black Scorpion.

Ekpedeme had contested in the Students Union Government for the position of President but lost twice, owing to what he described as "godfatherism". He was not in the good books of the institution's management, and the "king-makers" did not consider him "a chosen one" because with him on the seat as president, no money would be embezzled! In most of the solidarity rallies he had organised and led, he'd always denounced anti-student policies, like an astronomical hike in school fees. Even when the soft drink giant increased the bottle price of their products, he led a protest which forced the eviction of the soft drink giant and replaced it with their rival in the market. At the height of incessant killings arising from cult clashes, he came out and condemned the development, mentioning names of some cult members, students' sponsors, and their departments.

This very act was the icing on the cake as he was pencilled down for elimination. Many of our hit squads were in the same faculty with him, so Ekpedeme knew them well. I had watched him keenly over time and aspired to be like him. He was

149

a gifted Orator; his words were like sugar and the students, the ants that clung to it for life. His stage was the school premises, while the platform was any podium. I had declined to connive with our organisation, Black Scorpion, to deflate him. It was common knowledge that Ekpedeme would deliver a speech at the students' solidarity centre to herald the sports week; thus, my cult leaders believed it was a good day to make a hit on him.

That day, he had walked into the arena with his disciples. His many nicknames rented the air – *Eyen-isong, Akpan-Akanawan!* Soon he was ushered into a seat, and a standing ovation was given to him. He finally sat down, still looking defiant. Deep down, I knew the place would be stampeded, and my hero would bite the dust and bid the world farewell. A cream coloured Mercedez Benz pulled up on the opposite direction to Ekpedeme by the right side of the pavilion. Cold shivers ran through my body. I knew immediately that our agents of death were around. Terror alighted first, followed by two other unknown individuals, whom I had earlier come across as our hitmen from another institution.

I watched as these vicious guys strolled around surveying the area, and at that same time, a voice came through the loudspeakers announcing the programme of the day, signifying the official start of the event and got my heart beating faster. The opening prayer was offered, followed by a brief remark from the Dean of Students' Affairs. Then, it was time for the short speech, which everybody knew would be delivered by Etinan's own Martin Luther King, Jr. – Ekpedeme. When he was called to the podium, another standing ovation and loud cheers greeted his quick, long strides to the podium. He saluted the students in the usual solidarity fashion of the university and began his short speech:

"Fellow students, fellow adventurers in this Ivory Tower," he intoned, "I am immensely elated, humbled, and honoured to be the one chosen for this important speech. I must commend you all on your unalloyed support and understanding so far in the face of the challenges we face on our campus…"

I tuned out Ekpedeme's voice as my attention became focused on what was about to go down any moment from then. I saw Terror re-enter the car again, fumbling with something inside the car; I did not see the other two hitmen. I felt a need to help Ekpedeme, maybe alert him somehow, but I couldn't dare; we always had spies around whenever there was going to be such an attack. These spies' duty was to thwart any effort of tracing the attackers; they were to mislead and distort useful information that could lead to a possible arrest and prosecution. These same spies were around the venue in their numbers, also watching us for any sign of weakness. Since it was a school event within the campus, I knew that the spies would detect whatever effort that came through me that could prevent the hit from taking place and thus, the process of my elimination would hastily commence. I saw Terror re-park the vehicle such that the rear faced the podium while the front was directed to an escape route. Then, the two other hitmen appeared and also entered the vehicle; I was not sure what they were doing inside the car, but they seemed busy. Later, one of them came out and lit a cigarette, looking quite relaxed; they seemed to be buying time, maybe some unexpected hitch came up. Hopeful, I turned my attention once again to Ekpedeme's speech.

"...sport has always been a rallying point for social cohesions and unity," he said, "this unity should bind us in all our endeavours. We should unite and speak in one voice on issues like cultism, flagrant abuse of our right by the Nigerian police, indecent dressing among our female colleagues, and extortion in whatever guise by lecturers."

Applause rent the air at his bold words.

When the students quieted down, he continued, "Our future depends on those problems we jointly solve today. This is expected of us as future leaders, even at the risk of our lives—"

He was cut off mid-sentence. Several gunshots rang out simultaneously in rapid succession and pandemonium broke out in the pavilion; everybody scampered to safety. Those shots hit Ekpedeme; one on his forehead and others on stomach. There were other random shots meant to scare away anyone from the fleeing vehicle, which seemed to be the only suspect in the unfolding drama. But these supposedly random shots were done with such expert precision that three more bullets hit Ekpedeme; one in the middle of his chest, bursting crimson, and two on his upper torso, throwing his arms wide. The microphone in his hand flew to another direction. He fell backwards. His buttocks hit the ground first, then, slowly, his back, and in that instant, his eyes, wide open, connected with mine as if pleading, before his head fell backwards, or maybe it was my imagination because of the guilt I felt. At that moment, my heart stopped, and my mouth went dry, as my entire being shook from fear; I couldn't get my legs to move, I just stood there, moping. His head had jerked so violently, which I believe must have damaged his spinal cord. Just like that, he was sniped out of life!

All three of them pulled their triggers on "one" single young man like they were attacking an army. Everyone was screaming and running helter-skelter; a few ran smack into me, jolting me back to reality. The few policemen who came along with some dignitaries outran the dignitaries they were meant to protect; none was ready to take a bullet for his master or even protect anyone, for that matter, under such daring call of duty.

However, unlike such shootings in the past,

students immediately rushed to Ekpedeme's side, while a good number of others chased after the fleeing car on foot and motorbikes. Seeing the confusion, I quickly blended into the crowd, and finally, summoned up the courage to move closer to the podium without arousing suspicions from the Black Scorpion spies, and from the look of the unresponsive body, it was easy to tell that Ekpedeme had crossed to the other side, and his situation had become irredeemable. I realised then that I was the only person in the crowd who did not appear shocked by the event of the day; well, that would be because I was in the know, and also a part of the executioners.

First aid that was meant for the football match was used in a futile attempt to revive Ekpedeme; everybody around became emergency medical personnel. The Red Cross officials started retracing their steps from their designated area to the podium. Bandage, water, and plaster, even Varicose ointment was brought in. Though deep down I knew he was gone, I muttered prayers for Ekpedeme's survival. He was immediately rushed to a waiting car, which was provided by one of the students. The Efik traditional attire he adorned was torn into shreds and soaked in his blood. Some were fanning his lifeless body. Mouth to mouth resuscitation was adopted; I felt like screaming to tell them to give up the effort – he was no more. I watched as the vehicle conveying his corpse sped away and sympathising students trying to follow it. And sadly, the sports week became the "death week" as many other students caught in the crossfire were killed and some injured. The opening ceremony could no longer hold as Cables and wires used for the event began to undergo various processes of disconnection. I stealthily smuggled myself out of the crowd as the latecomers to the event continued to pour in to see things for themselves.

The following morning, all the State media houses relayed the sad incident; I heard the local Radio station, Etinan FM 105.3, news broadcaster say, *"Mr Ekpedeme Asanga is dead. He died of gunshot injuries he suffered at the sports pavilion of the University of Etinan by men suspected to be cultist…"*
I could not stand to listen to the horrid details, so I turned off the radio and remained indoors throughout the rest of the day.

By Monday morning, I entered the school using the second gate through the Faculty of Social Sciences. A notice board had Ekpedeme's picture in a three-piece suit smiling; he looked so alive, it felt eerily impossible that he was gone from the world, never to be seen ever again. Students gathered and were discussing the event. The stories were passed from one mouth to another, and each with different variations to it. Some said that it was the VC that ordered his elimination. Also, many of the academic staff that had had issues with him in the past were accused and suspected. And some said it was because he was nursing an ambition to contest in the next session's National Association of Nigerian Student (NANS) election. I heard a female student telling her friends that the assailants were in military fatigues, which were utterly false, of course. I did not need to correct such impressions since such were the needed stories to distort the real fact about our hit squad. There was no lecture that day, even lecturers that came to the campus were few; mourning hung over the school like a thick dark cloud, and before 3:00pm, the main campus that was always bubbling with activities was deserted.

The entire campus was awash with obituary pictures of Ekpedeme; everywhere I turned, his image was staring me in the face. Born 24years ago, got admitted into the institution to study medicine, he was in the 5th year or what we called 500 level. Nobody was sure whether he wanted to vie for any elective position in the SUG in his final year next session. Ekpedeme was a success story, rising from squalor, he developed himself by adding value to himself, self-trained and self-made; he, no doubt, would have made a fine medical doctor. His death was a loss, not only to the university community but also to the nation as a whole. He would be remembered as the rose that grew from the rock.

On the fifth day, a candlelight procession was

observed by students of the School of Medical Sciences in his honour. But it became an all-students' affair, not just students of medical sciences; students trooped out in their large numbers to bid farewell to one of their own that shone like a northern star in the citadel of the learning firmament. They marched in their black attires, candle in hands singing dirges, while some carried placards, condemning the atrocities and calling for the police to begin a full-scale investigation into the murder and bring the culprits to justice. However, I knew such would not happen because Terror and his friends got to safety, covering their tracks and destroying any clue that would have led to their arrest.

Moreover, the police had never succeeded in unravelling the mystery behind such high-profile killings in the past. Many human rights activists had also travelled this same road, and their killers vanished into thin air without any traces. Political killings had also been added to the lengthy list of unresolved murders. If I recall vividly, the floodgate of unsolved murders was flung open by a certain military junta, who had dispatched an American-trained frontline journalist using a letter bomb, and many years after his death, his killers were still walking shoulder high on the streets, unembarrassed and unmolested.

The security apparatus in the school was called into

question and insinuations had gone around that violence would break out during the procession. But this never happened. None of the sad faces seen around seemed interested in such reprisal as such would be regarded a sad and shameful departure from the deceased's belief in non-violent means of achieving set objectives.

The female students were the dominant gender in the crowd; their gloomy faces told the story well enough. No one wears an outward display of soft emotion like the female, but they're also unbeatable at being mean, and when they are mean, they are harder than stone – an impenetrable wall. The female members of the Black Scorpion are a living testament to this; sometimes I actually wonder if they have any heart beating within their chests at all – silent, smooth operators, rarely ever caught or even suspected. A few of these mean-spirited Black Scorpion females were in the crowd, emotionless, not to honour the dead but to seek out and mark any troublesome female students that as much as utter any wrong word against the cult. New students were also great in number as the deceased had touched their lives in various ways. Death, which is acclaimed as the ultimate end, was proved wrong on that day as Ekpedeme lived on and became more popular in death than when he was alive. His face and name were constantly in the media and on people's lips. There had existed a strong bond of love between him and the students; even I envied his new popularity that I felt like dying in the same manner. The procession would go down in the history of the institution as the longest ever because it stretched from the main campus down to the students' hostels and beyond a distance of three kilometres.

****

Three weeks later, memories of the brutal event of Ekpedeme's death seemed to have faded away, as worries or fears of any other attack vanished from the students' minds, which was evident in the return of normal campus nightlife once again. As for me, all feelings of guilt and dread were completely gone; I had bounced back to normal, and also gotten back into the good books of Capone and Bossman. Thus, Bossman sent me to a Scripture Union (SU) meeting to gather information for the Black Scorpion, so I had gone pretending to be a new convert. The programme continued long into the night, almost 10:00pm, and I got home disappointed, having gathered no tangible information. When I went out that night with Etete and others to a drinking parlour, I shared the irrelevant detail I had, so they know that I really went on the errand, affirming my loyalty to the organisation once again.

However, the next morning, I woke up with great

hope for a stress-free day, especially having just completed my term-papers in different courses the previous day. A short prayer was enough to gear my anxious being into motion. Oh yes; make no mistake about it and do not be surprised, we also do pray to the Almighty God. Like a tired dog that had just woken from slumber, I stretched and yawned before walking into the bathroom, which I shared with Etete; he didn't sleep in the apartment last night. I bathed like a typical Ibibio native fowl which dreaded water, throwing the cold water all around the floor in the process. The little soap left in the bathroom was not enough to meet the demands of my sweat-dried body, but I bathed, singing like "joy" was my middle name; I couldn't even understand what was making me feel so happy; maybe getting so "high" last night.

However, if I had known that what looked like a happy day would become the beginning of my nightmare, I would have at least listened to the inner voice, which on several occasions forewarned me about an impending disaster. It began with the lather from the soap getting into my eyes and burning like hot pepper. Then, I almost fell stepping out of the bathtub to the wet floor that I had splashed water all over. And in trying to find my balance, I hit my elbow on the sink and saw stars from the excruciating pain that hit my brain. All these seemed like warning signs, but my firm belief in the Christian doctrine made me discard such insinuations as wholly vested in superstition. I jumped into my black trousers and grey T-shirt, with the tenacity of a newly recruited infant soldier, and within fifteen minutes, the self-acclaimed son of a medical doctor was on his way to the History department.

On reaching the Faculty of Arts block, I met a crowd with tensed countenance discussing the event that had just happened earlier this morning. Hisses and sighs ruled their discussion, and eyes were piercing holes in my little being; I suspected some kind of trouble immediately. But never in my wildest imagination did the thought of me being seen as an accomplice occur to me. As I got to the class and walked to my seat, almost all the students around me lowered their voices, and some even pretended as if they were not looking at me, such that each time I caught the lily-livered students staring at me, they would quickly turn away their gaze. Fear seized my whole being, and for the first time in three weeks, I was afraid again. I knew something was wrong somewhere, but I couldn't put my finger on what. Perhaps, I was supposed to be in the know, to warrant this type of welcome this morning.

"He is their informer. That's the informer," rent the air, though in whispers.

A bold course mate amongst the gossip group approached me and muttered the morning greetings. I looked at him questioningly, wondering what was good about the morning with all the killer stares directed at me.

"My guy find your way o," he said in Pidgin English. Etop was his name.

"Etop, what is going on?" I asked, looking confused.

"Clans men don hit again o; four guys don die," he answered, folding his right thumb to indicate the number four, *"and all man dey suspect you; them say you don belong and say na your people do am, and say na you be their informer."*

The briefing descended on me like thunder on a rainy day. It hit me hard to my marrow; I felt the truth in what Etop had said. Everybody now knew that I was the one giving my clique information. No wonder the word "informer" was on their lips. Where do I run to? Everywhere seemed trap infested. It was like a web, a network of diabolical initiative. Sinister in plot, I felt like someone stranded in the desert without water. As at that morning, every student on my mind represented the image of a traitor; worst still, none of my bosom friends were around to deliver me from this doom. If I had wings, I would have flown to a safe distance, but here was I, trapped in an imaginary cage, a prison of seclusion. My conscience hurt severely, memories flooded my confused mind, and my vision became blurry.

So, Etete meant what he had told me about me in the school! The whole plot played out before me – straight in my retina. I realized that though I was afraid; I was more feared and dreaded by fellow students.

While I stood, seemingly emotionless, plotting my escape strategy, the students froze in fright as I turned to look out of the window. Etop went out to survey the vicinity for me; I wondered why he was trying to help me considering the popular belief that I was responsible for the demise of four students earlier that morning. I was well aware of the gravity of the deed, and the nation's law book could confirm that.

I remembered vividly in my drunken stupor the night before, how Etete entered the room looking angry; Capone, followed by one of the high-ranking hitmen, Ofege, who was also Etete's cousin, and two other young men I could not recall their faces; they looked overly serious. "Blood must flow" seemed to be the only phrase they spoke and understood. Surprisingly, they were not discussing in low tones as such discussions demanded; they argued and shouted unnecessarily. In some instances, some other names replaced their real names; too drunk to care, I had thought of it as being some fashionised botanical names. "Drunkenness is a bastard!"

How wrong I was! These aliases that my "dangerous" friends were calling themselves simply suggested devilish motives. Apparently, their devilish motives bred devilish intent and went on to execute a devilish purpose. Before six hours, FOUR souls had been dispatched to the land of the silenced ones.

As I stealthily slipped out of the classroom and exited my department with the help of Etop, my big head began to hurt and felt too heavy for my neck. Perspiration revealed its presence on my T-shirt and underwear. I felt like crying. I felt like confessing all I knew about the organisation to exonerate myself – I didn't do this!!! How dare they think I did it?! Just barely five months in the school with admission gotten through the back door, and already the university gates looked wide open for rustication for me, and accomplice to murder as the charge against me.

Feared engulfed me like fire as the thought occurred to me that in the corridors of power, both the high and the low do not know me or my parents, unlike Etete, whose intervention would be speedy and good to hang his fate on. Same could not be said for me, a wretched victim of greed and vain quest for power. I had become a prisoner of conscience doing time in between different prisons of fear.

In an effort to pull myself together and think clearly, I realised this news was what Nsa, our Informinua, was trying to tell me earlier when I ran into him on my way to the campus! He did say that Etete and his co-travellers had waylaid two students, a male and a female, early hours of this morning. The female student had embarrassed him at the former Governor daughter's birthday party when he requested a dance from the innocent girl, and the girl had also hauled insults at Ofege, who had touched her buttocks. But I was just too happy to pay attention to such negativity, so I quickly dismissed him without hearing the full details and rushed off to school. Gradually, it all began to make sense; the poor girl did not know she had majorly offended the demi-gods of the campus. And the penalty for an offence of that magnitude was forceful carnal knowledge of the girl – rape but could also be death if she further angered them in the process.

I was filled with dread; the thought of a "friend" of the former governor's daughter being one of the dead victims was terrifying; that's playing too close to a raging fire. Barely 19years old, I was too young to be caught in such a heated, ugly situation; I thought as I considered my low estate. It was like being stripped naked to see through all my cover ups; I looked so empty and worthless. My cheerful, smiling, bold face gave way to a mask of fear. I always thought we were the hunters, not knowing I would so suddenly become the hunted, or maybe I was always the hunted – I play by the cult rules, I get hunted by the students, and if I play against the cult rules, I get hunted by the cultists. Trust cultists with the apparatus of intimidation; I had become a pawn in their chess game. I dispatched threat letters to our would-be victim's abode and went on hits with Etete's Beretta M9 pistol, which had long become mine since Capone said I used it better than Etete, and so, asked me to keep it. I did the bidding of the cult with vigour, especially the delivery of threat letters.

I remember taking a letter to a house about forty-one kilometres away from the school in another state, and proudly declaring to the recipient, *"you've been served"*, in the way lawyers would say it, feeling like I had won a million-dollar lottery. Upon my return, Ofege had given me a congratulatory handshake, claiming that the latest "client", as we called our victims, was within reach. I noticed how his face brightened up with a satisfactory toothy smile after I had reeled out a perfect description of the location, which he confirmed. His pleasant looks were very misleading, and it betrayed the unassuming mind, just like mine did. But the students seemed to have finally seen through my innocent façade as my name took precedence on their lips, and they hunted me, albeit fearfully, for a deed I knew nothing about. Call me crazy, but it would seem I had been set up by my cult members to take the fall for this one; maybe to see how I would handle it.

I remember we had hopped into a Toyota Corolla driven by Ofege, from the apartment, after I got in from the SU meeting the night before; we went to a drinking parlour. There, almost everybody was congratulating themselves, except me, who stood looking confused; I was still in doubt on the reason behind the celebration. Indeed, my attitude was noticeable, to say the least. Terror had asked about my wellbeing, which I answered in affirmative. The two strangers among us seemed to have their eyes trained on me; perhaps, they were not comfortable with my mood. The strangers, from a renowned university from the south-west of the country, decided to test my manliness with marijuana, *"ikong-ekpo"* or *"igbo"* as we called the sliced grass. They gave it to me to wrap in their presence while they watched with keen interest, noting my expertise. I wrapped it neatly before requesting for a match box. The next test was for me to consume five bottles of beer. Timid and trembling, I was cowered into submission with no resistance whatsoever. Their influence over me was like covering a snail with a bowl; it can only move within the confines of the bowl but cannot escape – typical case of "no retreat, no surrender". All five green bottles of alcohol were popped open; the liquor foamed whitest over a sparklingly gold content, and the rising bubbles were fascinating to the eyes. I remember I was dropped at the apartment later that night. Though drunk, I could identify my room, and also saw them come into the room, screaming blue murder.

It turned out that Ofege and his cohorts had led the female student and her male companion at gunpoint to a deserted area by the road leading to the faculty of Arts, then first shot him point-blank on the forehead for freely having what the demi-gods wanted, and then tried to rape the girl; she was hysterical and fought them fiercely, preferring to die first than be raped by all five or any of them, for that matter. With all that fracas, two other male students returning from the night club, who had heard her screams and the gun shot came to her rescue; all three of them were shot dead.

I was a bit relieved to learn later that the girl was not a friend of the former governor's daughter; they didn't even know each other, but she had been invited to the party by another friend – not that it made her any less important nor her death deserving or less painful. They left the four dead bodies lying there like ghoulish mannequins and led all trails to me – the Black Scorpions had purposely leaked out my name to the students as a suspect.

After days of protests by the students, I was arrested, and a thorough investigation was carried out into the four murders by the police. Two days after my arrest, I was released on bail; Bossman posted my bail. I walked out of police custody with a swag, and a self-satisfied smirk at the officers. To fulfil protocol, I had to go into hiding to avoid any confrontation with the students, though the police had unlimited access to me. The officers kept coming at me unannounced, and each time they found nothing to pin me down; I simply sat back and smirked at them.
Three weeks later, the case was closed; no arrests were made, and I was cleared. I did not snitch on

the Black Scorpion. And by the way, leaking out my name as a suspect to the students was the Black Scorpion's twisted way of testing my loyalty to the cult. I didn't see that coming.

CHAPTER TEN

I rested my head in my hands with my elbows propped on my desk in class; the lecturer, Dr. Akpe, was droning on about *"History and Human Capital"*. What a night I'd had! These days, every night seemed to have something going on – either we were drinking and smoking high or gone on some violent nocturnal activity till the early hours. I just needed one unbroken night to sleep and still have some money, and I would be as good as new again. I raised my red laced eyeballs to look at the bespectacled man in the tweedy suit, thinking of how to escape from the boring class. I was too tired and in no mood for the lecture, and worst of all, too broke. Find me broke, and you'll find a useless fellow! Isn't life such an irony? I, who was accustomed to poverty all my life, got just a little taste of the wealthy life, and suddenly became too used to such luxuries.

I hated it each time I was broke, I had become accustomed to money, which made it an easy motivation to do whatever it took to get it. And at this time everyone was broke; not a single one of us had any money. The funny thing was that money was elusive to us most of the time – no thanks to our reckless spending habits; we had our financial droughts. So funny was this particular financial woe that even Etete was affected; he was completely empty. While Uko, one of Capone's bodyguards, *obtained* from his numerous protégé to cater to himself and Capone, others were constantly without. It could be that they were all relying on Etete, just like I did. So, when the idea of getting money was presented, I was conscripted without a second thought, and I also willingly accepted without any thought.

Hence, while Nsa gathered and cleaned our guns, I went to carry out surveillance of the target location. For three whole days, I was on stakeout duty around the area to ascertain that our attack point and escape route, which was a major strength in our operations, were safe. And stakeout duty meant hanging out under the blazing hot sun with a hungrier stomach. But because I had proven myself to be good in the perfect analysis of our target locations after every surveillance, this daunting task was always assigned to me.

The day finally dawned, and we all rounded up at Terror's, where we had agreed to meet and set out from on the business of the day. The Black Scorpion ladies had delivered enough food to his place for all of us – that was part of their duty whenever we had operations like this. We ate very well; every one of us was well-fed. We usually do this because it could be the last meal for any of us or all of us. Going by experience with such assignments in the past, some never returned alive. Apart from that, most times during these kinds of assignment, there was no place or time to get any edibles, and we never know how long the operation would take. So, we ate one of the best prepared *Edikang Ikong* and washed it down with some green bottles of alcohol blended with *Ikong Ekpo*; I guess we overdid it this time around, as it took its toll on us – we all fell into a deep sleep in Terror's room; the only movement we did was to adjust ourselves properly on the floor to escape suffocation because we had clustered together in the room, and some were releasing terrible farts.

Hours later, I woke up to a dark reality – it was 8:15pm. The evening breeze that filtered into the room through the open horizontal louvres of the window played two vital roles for me. First, it was helping my friends to adjust themselves to another round of snoring. Secondly, it helped air out the room of the detestable farting competition. Anyway, I woke up to discover Terror did not sleep much for unknown reasons; we exchanged glances occasionally that spoke volumes, meaning that he was conscious of his environment and thus, kept watch while we slept, leaving ourselves vulnerable. I found one aspect of him intriguing though – five bottles of alcohol and some wraps of *Ikong Ekpo* did absolutely nothing to his system. I sat up, now wide awake, in silence with him, but after several minutes of wishful thinking and unresolved desire, I got up to release some excess liquor in my system. I navigated his off-campus bungalow, left, right and around, searching for the toilet, and soon realised the toilet was at the back, outside the house, and it was a pit toilet – latrine! I'll be damned; Terror, British born, rich boy, a latrine?!!! The place was suffocatingly stinky; I covered my nose. I bet the darkness must have sent the flies away, though I could still hear a few buzzing. I unzipped my black jeans, and missing the toilet hole, I wet the surrounding grounds, with it foaming like some beverage. I stepped out, careful not to step on anything unpleasant, and went back to the room. There, I met the remaining four sitting up and yawning like hungry dogs. We revived our discussion, which we were meant to have finished hours ago, but instead, we ate and fell asleep like fools; thus, we spent about an hour strategising, and drew up a perfect attack plan. I explained the location to them once more, making sure to point out the entry and exit routes clearly.

I also briefed them about other escape routes, should the need arise. At the end of that discussion, we began smoking again to kill time before our departure. A local brew of *"Ufofop"* was our companion this time around. The next stage was to encourage ourselves; Terror spoke to us like a platoon leader, but of course, our adventure was like embarking into a battle. He demonstrated to us the different loading processes of each gun, and we paid rapt attention as though our lives depended on it; well, I guess it did.

At about 11.45pm, Nsa announced his presence by his signature tap on the door and walked in to inform us that the vehicle was outside waiting for us. Outside the compound, we met one other friend in the organisation and had a little introduction. A piece of red cloth was torn into long pieces, and a piece was given to each of us, which we tied around our head the moment we began the operation. We all looked forward to a better life after the operation. Everything was going smoothly that night, and we thought that we would become young millionaires by the time "the business", as we called our criminal adventure, was over. Uko, who had been silent all along, spoke softly and thoughtfully that we must create fear in our victims to suppress them and earn their respect. Since we were targeting state-of-the-art luxury cars and brand-new SUVs. We promised our victims an ordeal of a lifetime.

Through his father's connection, Etete had arranged two serving police officers that would help us escort the vehicles to the buyers. We set up a roadblock at a hidden place as was advised by the policemen, knowing that one of the civic responsibilities of the citizens was to be law-abiding. So, submission into stopping would not pose any problem since the roadblock was at a place the police had used before the ban on checkpoints by the Inspector General of Police. As such, I knew that even though we may appear suspicious, most police officers around the country were yet to adhere to the roadblock ban. Thus, we all felt that those people who would be well aware of this responsibility would not find it difficult to submit to our pseudo search. The civil responsibility to obey, however, would convey potential victims on a face-to-face encounter with us.

At 1:00am, we arrived the target location, outskirts of Etinan town, adorned in our perfect disguise – black clothing sewn in the police-style fashion to take the form of police officers. At Okut Ikang junction, directly opposite where our car was parked, was a Jeep Grand Cherokee SUV and a salon car in the distance driving towards us graciously. We had waited endlessly before these attractive vehicles appeared, so, we were not ready to gamble, especially when a white man was spotted in the passenger seat of the SUV. The sighting of a foreigner meant this was a good catch for us. His embassy would soon be briefed about his kidnap, and we can, therefore, initiate a profitable negotiation that would lead to a rewarding ransom.

While we waited patiently to pounce on our prey, the driver of the SUV was quick enough to discern that we were not real police officers, as he realised that the police had not blocked this spot for a long time. And having found themselves facing a den of armed bandits, who were disguised as police officers, they were not going to relent on escaping from us. So, as the driver of the SUV slowed down for an eventual manoeuvre, I charged at them threatening to open fire if they don't stop for searching. My comrades in crime barked furiously at them, and within a few seconds, the two vehicles were in our custody. We demanded their vehicle's license and other particulars, and though they met all requirements, it was not in our best interest to let them go. Cargos like this are worth millions, after all, that was what brought us to the spot in the first place. Etete accused the white man of being a spy, and the rest of us took the accusation to a whole new level. The driver of the Salon car tendered his particulars as well but unknown to him, we were after the occupant he was carrying, a very high-profile personality. The white man started to plead and explained that he was a construction expatriate, not a spy, insisting that we should take him to our police station, and he would contact a legal representative to prove his innocence. Poor, clueless guy; I thought, holding back from laughing.

However, determined not to be held hostage by criminals, the second man in the SUV that sat beside the white man at the back, opened the right-side door of the SUV and hit me on my chest, sending me crashing to the ground; I guess he was not as scared as we thought. On reflex, Nsa grabbed a gun and opened fire; this left us all shocked momentarily, being the first time for him to ever fire a shot at anything, let alone an intimidating, huge, human being; though he missed. Before I could get up, the man grabbed Nsa, after first covering him with the wide Agbada outfit he was wearing and dealt Nsa such brain-numbing blows repeatedly before I got up and punched the man hard in the abdomen, finishing it with a solid uppercut to his jaw. As he staggered backwards, Nsa shot him, and the tall figure fell to the ground screaming to be spared.

On seeing his blood soaking his clothes, I thought the man would soon give up the ghost. We quickly ran towards our colleagues who were having difficulty overpowering another vehicle that was ahead of us. The injured man proved our judgment of him wrong by tearing into the bush for an escape that shocked Nsa to a frozen position. "So, you didn't shoot him to die?" I yelled at Nsa.

He did not respond; he just stood there, staring at the bush, dumbfounded.

Before the man disappeared into the thick bush, I noticed he was limping with much strength, and at that, I realised our kidnap operation could be in great jeopardy if the man got help immediately, and the morning was gradually dawning; it was almost 4:00am. With a situation like this on our hands, time was everything; besides, it was almost a two-hour drive back to town; thus, we ordered the rest of our victims out of both vehicles and transferred them into the different vehicles to avoid further complications. The white man sat in between Uko and Etete, with Nsa in the front seat in our car, driven by our resident driver, Inyene; their vehicle trailed behind the Jeep driven by Terror, with Bossman, the two captured drivers, and the friend of the organisation – can't remember his name, while the Salon car, driven by our guy, Ndiana, conveyed the others and me.

Our prized captive, the white man, was the visiting Director of Triple Alpha Construction Company Plc, Cross River State. Also held captive by us were Chief Nkutang, a seasoned Estate Surveyor, and the new manager of the company, south of

Niger, Mr. Offiok Nduyo. Both men were on their way to inspect a newly acquired site for the proposed ultra-modern factory when we struck.

Though the visiting director we abducted was valuable, he also became our nemesis. We could not go far with him because his Caucasian complexion exposed our act when the vehicle that he was being conveyed in got stopped for a routine check at a legitimate roadblock into Calabar. In this case, the police were not meant to search the vehicle, but I want to believe that the mere sighting of the white man was enough reason for them to play to the gallery and search, in hopes of getting a few naira notes as tip. It was almost 6:00am, and the morning sun was already peeking out; it was bright enough to see our faces. One of the police officers, after sternly staring at all of us declared that we were under arrest. That moment, I knew that we had lost this rare opportunity to make it big. But Black Scorpions are not known to *come last*, so, we started demanding reasons for them to arrest "fellow" colleagues. What we didn't think about was that most of us had beards, which was one of the cardinal appearances against the ethics of the police profession, and most of us knew next to nothing in security and policing. Thus, the few questions that were thrown at us opened the lid for the police officers.

I used all kinds of foul language, trying to maintain a courageous "police officer" temperament, while scanning for an escape route that we never anticipated in that part of the town. Sensing trouble, one of the police officers cocked his rifle and opened fire into the air, but I was no longer scared. After so many weeks of being hunted, every action for me was automatic, reflexive, efficient; right now, escaping was my top priority, and for effective clarity of thought, I needed to drop all fear. I already knew the police officers wanted us alive; they also wanted to rescue our captives to make a bold statement, and then parade us before television cameras as captured criminals. The way I saw it; we simply were university cult boys having fun; I couldn't let them parade me to the world as a criminal.

We all got down from the vehicles, including our captives as ordered by the policemen. Our expensive Berreta M9 pistol and a cheap locally made double-barrel gun that we'd cut to size was another blunder, which the police quickly noticed. Our numbers were few compared to about seventeen policemen, all armed. Now, I had a bad feeling this was more than a search for a mere tip; the escaped limping man must have tipped them off. Why else would there be so many police officers in one place at once? So, eight misguided youngsters, whose courage was based on drugs, buzz and quick money, with only four guns, were nothing before them. I had dropped the gun I was carrying inside the vehicle to emerge clean in the event of arrest by the police. Immediately we got down from the car, the white man started singing like a bird that we had them arrested. I paced back and forth, getting ready for a dash; a race that would set me free from another close shave with the law or death within a short space of time.

I took the first steps with all vigour, sprinting away like a man fleeing from wild creatures. I looked back to see a police patrol car close behind me as I moved into the direction of a fish market before me. I felt a hand trying to grab me, but I was too fast, or maybe it was just providence. As I ran, I heard different gunshots, and a few bullets flew past me in the same direction. The rapidity of the gunfire stopped as abruptly as it started. The early morning market was already open and buzzing with life; thus, the market women and customers screamed and

182

scampered into safety; I guess that was why the gunshots stopped. By this time, I was in the midst of the market, trying to blend into the confused crowd, while tearing off my fake police shirt, leaving an old green T-shirt that I had worn under the black shirt. The women started cursing the policemen soon after the gunshots stopped, and I stealthily walked away.

CHAPTER ELEUEN

The last couple of days, I had been resigned to a dark season under a dense cloud sheet, fearfully laying low; then, all of a sudden, that didn't even matter anymore. I had a ray of God-given sunshine at my door as I finally came out of hiding. Whatever magic Capone, along with Etete and Terror's parents worked, paid off, as all our guys held in custody, and me, who was on the WANTED list for "armed robbery", got cleared and released with all charges dropped.

"Phew, that was a close one! We got out free, yet again; just like that!"

Although these arrests were attracting much unpalatable attention to me from my course mates and other students in school, and it should, rightfully, make me ashamed, yet, all the easy and free pass we got at every wrong turn, got me more confident and trusting of the power of the organisation; thus, I waxed stronger and became more open to taking bigger chances. Even more so as the Black Scorpion Zonal Convention was coming up, where I had an opportunity to get noticed by some of the organisation's higher powers if I played my cards right; this was my first cult convention.

I had heard different stories of "conventions" of different clubs and organisations. It might interest you to know that the word convention in our parlance meant "wild party" or sometimes initiation in the most unlikely places, and it always comprised of ten or more institutions coming together. The number depended largely on the strength of such geographical zone. At the Black Scorpion convention good vibes flowed like a virus, but a good virus. There was already fun in the air, all hyped up and ready to give everyone a good time. The appeal of the convention made my synapses jump like beans in a tin. I couldn't be more alive if I were shouting from a high pile of money. The expected array of activities was like a drug that got me higher until my mind buzzed with pure joy. I felt as if my soul would shine so bright that my dark skin would start to glow like a light bulb, and my mind would become visible to all. I was so looking forward to this, and we all had money again, courtesy of some *runz* Capone pulled off with one of his wealthy uncles.

All the members were heavily taxed for the event; we all paid, and some voluntary contributions were also received. The convention was taking place at Ugep, which was about three or four hours away from Etinan; for members at the University of Etinan, it was also like our own special form of excursion, and so, we made arrangements for two luxurious airconditioned buses from the leading interstate transporter. Assorted alcoholic liquor and some bottles of water were purchased for the trip. Edible food items were also part of our luggage, though in smaller quantity.

The day of the convention finally dawned; we assembled at the designated place very early in the morning at 5:30am and departed for Ugep about 45 minutes later, so that we could arrive in good time to relax and prepare for the event later that night. We drove toward the northern part of Cross River State. After reaching Ugep L.G.A, we disembarked from the bus and walked a treacherous bush path down to the river. Etete and Terror moved faster and far ahead, expertly maneuvering the route better than the rest of us, and so, were already at the bank of the river waiting with some other members from another university. There was no formal exchange of pleasantries as we were ordered to enter the Canoe with an outboard engine. As more comrades turned up, we filled three of the four chartered boats and sailed off into the Calabar River. Our destination was a sand bar in the middle of the river towards Ikom, and we sang different songs, shouting on top of our voices as we sailed on.

Meanwhile, the boat was shaking violently in the waves; the current was so high that evening that it forced the boat driver to slow down at intervals in order to manoeuvre the waves easily. Despite the dangerous waves, drinks were popped open and freely consumed in one of the three boats, sailing gloriously on an ignoble errand. The convention euphoria consumed many of us, if not everybody, as the boats glided wearily against the high tides. One of the students with us happened to be good in marine geography and was also from the riverine area; so, he began to feed us with short tales about treacherous waters. Then, suddenly, he suggested a peculiar format to the boat driver to adopt, which the driver tried immediately, and it worked.

At this time, we were all intoxicated with liquor. I was so drunk that I wondered how I would be able to make it on my feet when we got ashore. The journey from the shore to the sand bar – Ugep Island was another 15 minutes' walk, according to the boat driver; it was not motorable. But because of the current, he estimated that we might likely spend 45 minutes before we got there, as the water would have covered most of the walking path, making it muddy and slippery; thus, difficult to walk. This water was dark green in all ramifications with all sorts of garbage swimming along with the current – nylon bags, rags, woods, excreta, up-rooted shrubs, and anything else you can think of as ugly, speeding past our boats. I recalled a time as children, we were burdened by the tales of the river being infested with wild reptiles. The excessive liquor in my system fanned that memory to the present as my mind staged an image of crocodiles crawling into the water at the shore, coming to eat us alive. With a slight quiver, I quickly shook off the thought, convincing myself it was not so and that my imagination was only playing tricks on me. But the liquor was gaining ground and taking over major functions of my body, and so, kept me seeing things that weren't there, including a huge killer-fly on my face, which made me give myself a head-spinning slap to everyone's shock and later got them laughing so hard at me because there was no killer-fly on my face. Well, that slap helped get my senses straight a little bit.

Two of the boats got to the shore before our own, and they all had to wait for us. Twenty minutes after, our boat, which was the biggest of the three boats with more students, roared and died away, granting the boat a smooth anchor and perfect bath when it docked at shore. We jumped out of panic, afraid to fall into the deep side of the water. Although some jumped into the wet sand, others jumped into knee-deep water. I held on to the wooden seat and carefully crawled out of the boat. There was laughter once again when I staggered into the water, and it was apparently clear that I was drunk. Etete walked towards me to observe me before also bursting into laughter. Others joined him, and I stood there laughing at the situation I found myself. And the party began from there; songs and shouts precluded other activities, and this noise could be heard miles away in the calm evening; it was already 4:45pm. I thought we would tone it down a bit, so as not to attract attention because two villages across the river were at war with each other; this communal conflict stemmed from the tussle about the clan throne. But none of us gave that any serious consideration.

Suddenly, I heard a voice in our midst barking down instructions to everyone, after which I was told that I would be punished for misbehaving. It was painful to be the one selected amongst the drunken lot for punishment. I took it with deep resentment for the Zonal Butcher, Boma Seriake, who dished out the order. The penalty was to off-load the entire luggage we came with for the convention from the boats. I folded my jean trousers and waded into the water with a gloomy face. The liquor in my system gave me the nerve to bear the punishment, and it acted like a cover shielding my face from scornful eyes. At this time, water was poured frequently on my head to reduce the effect of the liquor. After I had gotten everything ashore, Etete came back and dropped some pills into my palm, which he urged me to swallow. I did not question him on the ailment the pills were meant to cure, trust and familiarity made me delete that idea the very moment it started to form in my *medulla oblongata.* As far as I was concerned, Etete would not give me a substance that would do any harm to my system. Such was the relationship that existed between us; I simply had a feeling that those pills were to reduce the effect of the excess alcohol in my body.

Just when I thought that my predicament was over, another senior fellow in the organisation suggested that I should join the boat back to pick up other needed items we had left behind due to the boat insufficient capacity. An argument ensued over the issue as it was already beginning to get dark; Etete intervened, but the instruction prevailed. I had to go, so Etete decided to accompany me with the excuse that he intended to pick his bag from where he hid it at the riverbank. The boat driver pulled a rope, and the outboard engine came alive once again; I stepped in, followed by Etete and two other students I saw for the first time. The boat made a turn and began tearing down the water back to the riverbank. This time the current was in our favour; there was no difficulty of any kind. I turned and directed my stare at the party ashore; many of them had started hugging the girls amongst us. Shirts and blouses had given way to bare skin and bra. Shortly after, I saw them pick up their luggage and began the walk to the sand bar – Ugep Island, some with their arms around a girl. Deep down, I regretted what I was missing.

As for Etete, I knew he wanted to be around me in the event another punishment was suggested so that he could intervene; I thought to make an effort to appreciate him, but I changed my mind when I noticed that his face had this cold, solemn expression. His eyebrows twitched to join each other, giving him a brutish look, while the eyeballs dimmed in a less concerned manner; his teeth clenched in his mouth and the cheek muscle contracted, bearing witness to his mood. He was probably upset that his intervention was not regarded and so easily dismissed. Etete was a good friend, but he was more like a brother than a friend. Since we knew each other, whenever I was in any need that required his assistance, I always saw a passion and great desire in him to bring an end to whatever my trouble was. He was a problem solver. But our problem-solving tool was a revolver, which had become our girlfriend. He'd actually accompanied me because he felt that some of our guns might be missing as he personally supervised our last operation. While on our way, we heard several gunshots from our comrades. I began to gather myself as the drink was reducing its effect on me because of the pills Etete gave me. It was getting darker now; the moon was rearing its head in the horizon. Its gleaming ray split into stars as it touched the water in a straight line to its origin. The boat driver was shouting each time he talked, and because he was still inaudible, he slowed down the speed of the boat despite the approaching darkness, and we could hear ourselves once more.

He informed us that he was from the area, Itigidi to be precise. We also confirmed our fears about the communal conflict when he said that it was yet to be resolved. We lied that we were on a picnic and wanted to conclude it with this adventurous party. We all became lively again after that chat, but Etete was still in a pensive, mute mood all the way. The silence was back again till we got to the riverbank; I was uncomfortable because Etete was unhappy. I felt he had been put through a lot for my sake, and there was no better time than now for me to show appreciation, and probably sympathise with him; thus, I collected his wet shoe and removed mine before wading into the water when we anchored at the bank. As we were heading toward the main road, he glanced at his wristwatch, and I suggested that we should hurry, so as not to miss the fun. Jogging was not Etete's favourite pastime, especially now, so he declined the idea. No human being was on the road except moving vehicles which sped past. Later, we saw two figures approaching; a few steps further, the figures turned out to be Terror and Nsa, who had gone to hide our guns.

Back at the riverbank, we waited for another boat to take us back to the shore, where we would then find our way to the sand bar to join the others for the main event of the night – the convention. Etete was pacing up and down, murmuring to himself and sighing at intervals. While waiting at the riverbank, we could still hear sporadic gunshots coming from the sand bar. Time was running out, and our plan for the convention was beginning to appear quite bleak – no longer to materialise. Etete looked at his watch once more with the aid of the moonlight, and it was some minutes before 9:00pm. The last boat had departed, and none may likely come at this ungodly hour. He moved away, calling us to follow him and forget about the convention; we sadly obeyed without any argument. Besides, it was also an opportunity to vacate that mosquito-infested environment. Along the road, however, we were lucky to get a bus, which we joined to wherever. Only two seats were available, so we decided to lap one another. Since I was the first to enter the vehicle, I chose to lap Etete; Terror followed, and he lapped Nsa. Before we decided to alight at a popular junction in the community, the bus had driven for about twenty minutes, which meant we were, at least, twenty minutes away from the river that led to Ugep Island, where our comrades were – that was far enough and good enough for us.

As always, Etete took the lead while we followed until we entered a dark compound, full of tall trees, dimly lit by a lantern, which sat on a low stool at the veranda; the house was an old type. No one was outside, and it didn't seem like anyone was in the house, but luckily, we heard voices – these were Etete's cousins, Ofege's younger siblings; we walked in on them discussing the recent increase in cocoa prices at various markets in the community. After a series of pleasantries were exchanged, including extended hug between Etete and his aunt, Ayuk, we were offered old palm wine, which was the only edible item available in the house at that time of the night as everything had been consumed during dinner two hours earlier. Watching them, I sat wondering why his aunt lived in such poverty with her husband, while Etete's father lived in so much affluence. Well, maybe her husband was one of those proud ones who wouldn't accept help from his rich brother-in-law – stupid man; I thought. Anyway, being left without a choice and a nagging desire to fill the stomach, we accepted their offer of the old palm wine half-heartedly, but the fermented liquor only left a sour taste in our mouth and turned up the hunger pang, which we quietly had to endure through the night.

There are days the dawn proceeds as if it were not ready to come, yet schedule demands an entrance, and so the sun rises all the same, albeit half-heartedly with only a little bit of light; thus, it was still sufficiently dark when I felt someone tapping my shoulder, announcing it was morning and asking me to wake up. I grudgingly opened my eyes; it was Etete, and behind him stood a little boy of about 10years old with a broom in his hand; he was waiting for me to get up so he could sweep and arrange the room. That was when I realised where I was; though we were visitors, our liberty was limited if not restricted, so I hurriedly got up and stepped aside for him to do his morning chore. Etete was already fully dressed and appeared like he had gone out earlier.

Outside the compound, we exchanged greetings

with the extended family, especially the women and the aged amongst them, who had gone to sleep before we arrived the night before. Fresh palm wine was brought for us this time, while preparations for the morning breakfast was underway. A few hours later, a middle-aged man rode into the compound on a rickety bicycle with a sad tale. The day had looked beautiful, but little did we know that it was not going to be that way for many families. The man jumped down from the weather-beaten bicycle, leaving the iron and rubber to fall carelessly on the ground.

"The worst has happened," he announced, placing both hands on his head as he came closer to where we were all seated. His misty eyes, searching frantically for both cause and answer to the incident.

"You people are still sitting there and looking at me," he asked rhetorically, "And you people are drinking this early morning when the river is full of dead bodies."

At the mention of corpses, Etete and Terror stood up immediately, looking bewildered, while Nsa and I froze on our seats, eyes wide open, looking at one another. The man went to the backyard and announced the tale again, but in their native language, to the women preparing breakfast in the kitchen. Trust women; they began to shout and bounce up and down on their feet, loosing and retying their wrappers now and then. The women's drama was so much that I thought the man's information was narrated with more clarity, and so, better understood in their language, or perhaps the talebearer rephrased his tale differently. All eyes around were staring at us – the guests, in disbelief with mouth agape. So, we asked one of the cousins who then properly explained the import of the deaths that had occurred at the river to us.

"Who is behind this abomination? Who has committed this sacrilege?" The man asked nobody in particular, but his ghoulish look was piercingly on us.

We all kept quiet, staring at one another; I wondered why they all had their eyes trained on us; as far as I know, we didn't kill anyone.

"Even the civil war was not like this. Young men and women dying in droves like this in a time of peace; I have never seen anything like this before," he continued, snapping his long, bony fingers and folding his hands across his chest interchangeably.

The look on his face buried our thoughts; none of us could fathom it. What was the man actually saying? This was how mental illness starts; I thought. Because from all indication, the man looked like someone who needed psychiatric assistance. He was like a man obeying the prodding of a demon. With nothing more to say or do, he strolled out of the compound with both hands on his head, murmuring only-God-knows-what.

At mealtime, Etete suggested that we go and check on our comrades at the riverbank, and possibly join them back to school. Thereabout, a Cocoa Van drove into the compound with his uncle, and we helped off-load the bags of Cocoa from the vehicle. Since the driver was going our direction, we joined him and bade farewell to everybody. On getting to the junction that led to the river, we were greeted by a throng of sympathisers there. We continued down the slope to the river, seeing more people weeping uncontrollably, while others shrugged their shoulders and spat on the ground. Immediately we descended the slope, an ugly sight caught our attention, which sent jitters down our spine. More than twelve bodies were arranged at the riverbank. Many more were being removed from the water; it felt like a scene from a horror movie – our colleagues were all dead!

On our right hand, towards a place I would call the boat park, about eight corpses were lined side by side each other, their legs submerged in water. Etete called my attention to the water, and to my amazement, I saw human bodies in free swim towards the shore; most had their faces downwards in the water, while the others lay on their backs, and their faces stared up at the cloudy sky as if asking for explanations. At this point, we needed no prophet to tell us – the corpses were our colleagues that came for the convention; there were no locals amongst them, and there were also bullet injuries on their bodies while some drowned. These were university students like us – little wonder the talebearer and others at the house kept looking at us questioningly. Their looks were questioning how we came to be in the house at this same time and what we knew or was hiding about the incident.

But we knew nothing except that the boat drivers had told us that two communities across the river had an unresolved communal conflict, and none of us treated that information with the seriousness it needed. Each community had thought the other was about to attack them the eventful night of the convention; they had seen us trooping into the area in buses and concluded that we were mercenaries. The gunshots fired by our colleagues were misconstrued to mean an attack against them, and they, in turn, responded promptly. Both communities across the river shot at our comrades; many died in the crossfire as shelling was from both sides. There were bullet wounds even on the hapless female victims. A little further down, I saw the body of Etop, my course mate – he was to be initiated that night, then our Capone, Udofia, and the Zonal Butcher, Boma, who ordered that I should be punished, thereby saving my life in the process. Goosebumps covered my whole body at the reality of my close shave with death once again. Udofia was shot on the abdomen, while the Zonal Butcher had no injuries; it was evident that he drowned. His eyes were almost popped out of the sockets, wide open; his stomach was enlarged after gulping large quantities of water; his left hand had clutched a piece of deadwood, and the fingers of his right hand spread out in apparent desire to clutch something in his last few minutes. Terror and Nsa, stood at the riverbank, arms folded across their chests, shocked and speechless; I guess they're thinking the same thing as I was – we had all narrowly escaped this gruesome appointment with death.

Another boat arrived with four more bodies. We walked towards it, and behold, the only female corpse in this set of bodies was that of Etete's girlfriend, Ekaette, his latest catch, whom he was really fond of and cared for deeply. The girl was not the social kind, so, I wondered how Etete convinced her to join us on this trip. Now, she had met her untimely death. The last corpse to be removed lay face down, a greater part of the face submerged in the water inside the boat. As the corpse was being dragged off the boat, we noticed that there was a scorpion tattoo on the left shoulder just like that of Ofege. On a closer look, we saw the corpse was Ofege. Immediately, Etete broke down into uncontrollable tears – two people very dear to his heart, dead on the same day; it was too much to bear. Nsa and I held him as he doubled over in a loud wail, comforting him; he eventually calmed down, and being left without a choice, he wiped his eyes and got up on his feet again, staring into space.

Moreover, in our organisation, we do not shed tears over a dead colleague; it is the consequence of what we signed up for when we joined the Black Scorpion. Etete lost his cousin, Ofege, and his girlfriend, Ekaette, along with a host of others. The villagers commenced a search on the bodies to ascertain their identities. This yielded some success for them as some pockets had crisp Naira notes in different denominations. Students' identity cards of five different tertiary institutions were also recovered. With heavy hearts and a deep sense of loss, four of us departed from there and began our journey back to school. We also vowed not to disclose any information and the level of our involvement with the students.

Chapter Twelve

Death wasn't nice; I knew that already – we played its tunes and made others dance to it. It snatched wherever it could, taking people who were far too young, though these young ones called it to themselves. It didn't pretend to care, and it didn't pretend to distinguish; it took all available and swept them all like dirt into the river. It was supposed to be a fun outing for the Black Scorpions – "the" Zonal Convention; our party, where death had no seat! That was why Etete had hidden away our guns so that no one got drunk and became gun-happy amidst us!

As the days passed, I sat in my room, staring for hours, face sunken, my mind cold and haunted by memories of the dead bodies of my colleagues lining the riverbank like fallen dominoes, and the uncanny actions leading up to my escape from death; I could have been one of those dead ones but for that "punishment". And all for what? Even to that seemingly simple question, I couldn't give myself a reasonable answer. I began to review my earlier perspective of rock-solid confidence and trust in the power of the organisation; the impression that we could get away with anything – my colleagues couldn't get away with this one, not even Capone, and the consequence came with such finality, it's irrevocable! I felt deeply troubled within; I felt sorrowful, even though I was not particularly mourning anyone; not even those that died. It was the fear; the fear of the unknown was more unsettling and worse than the death itself. The population of the school was thinning away gradually because of cult activities, and we, Black Scorpions, were mostly responsible for that. I seldom went to lectures anymore, and whenever I did, I would return home almost immediately – so much for gaining admission into the school. The feeling of guilt and vulnerability hit me hollow.

Before joining the organisation, we were told of the connections that abound for being a member. I swallowed this bait hook, line and sinker. Today, the reality has dawned, and I have been disconnected like a failed system. I felt like an orphan, and my life seemed to be ebbing away. Extinction swamped my mind, and I was gradually journeying into ghost land. Etete, my bosom friend, had neither returned to school nor the off-campus apartment we shared since that day at the riverbank, and he was never found at his family home each time I stopped by to check on him. This forced me to withdraw further into my lonely shell. The days had become longer while the nights always stretched into eternity. Death seemed to stare me boldly in the face; I had lost count of the number of my colleagues that had passed to the great beyond, and at the same time, the faces of our victims kept reappearing to me – from the initiation ground to the unfortunate zonal convention, especially in their final moments, revealing how they wept and wailed, helpless and hapless till they died. Most of them returned to the infernal world with unfulfilled dreams; they departed the world with unique talents decayed in the belly of the earth, and with the solutions to our problems that they had come bearing.

As if suddenly remembering I was in the university for a purpose, I reluctantly got out of bed, where I had been sitting head in palms, to do a little reading to get rid of the troubled memories that besieged my soul. The notebook I opened stared back at me; I went through six pages but could not recall nor understood what I had read. I decided to tune off and ignore the world but there was no comfort for mean souls as they would meet their nemesis. I was guilty but I wanted to prove myself innocent; I was the wrong firewood in the hearth, so I could not bring me any warmth in the cold days. I remained silent, and this silence became a bond of friendship between me and the room.

The emotional lacerations I had was enough to put me in a state of perpetual cataclysm. All my dreams and aspirations were gradually being consumed in wasteful fatalities before my eyes. I was tempted to descend to suicide as I could not visualize any other escape route. The desire to prepare my own meal was no longer there. Even to go to my favourite eatery became a difficult task to accomplish; instead, local gin became my constant companion.

Children from the other apartments, playing outside did not help matters. Most times, they would knock at my door to enquire if I would like to send them on an errand when all I wanted to do was to be left alone. Not that I blame them;

they were great beneficiaries of these errands as the change from whatever amount of money I sent them with always became theirs. But one of them particularly was not helping the situation – the youngest of them, Abasiama, who was only six years old and quite small for his age. He had grown quite fond of me, and I also him, so, he was always at my door to report whoever beat him to me, and these days, no matter how long I ignored him, he wouldn't leave until I came out, listened to him and told him sorry, albeit absentmindedly. His elder brother was 10years old and was also in the habit of reporting to my doorstep every morning, but to drop a bottle of Ufofop – local gin, from his mother's shop, which I couldn't ignore. After that, he would hurriedly disappear to inform his mother that he had made a sale, and each time I received the item and paid him, I told him to keep the change, which made him more zealous. I drank, and my life ebbed away.

Oddly enough, going to my door each day to listen to the little boy and tell him sorry introduced some semblance of purpose to my existence, and I began to find strength gradually. Then, came this particular night that was a bad one; I couldn't sleep a wink, at least other nights I managed to get three hours or a little more of sleep after drinking myself to stupor, but not this one night. I laid in bed for the first time since the river deaths, thinking "productively" of what I had to do. Laying there in the dark, my hands had started to tremble from craving more drinks, and my throat felt dry and tight as a result of no food substance passing through it for some days, such that it was difficult to breathe and swallow saliva. My mouth also felt dried, and it felt like a lump was stuck in my gut. Thus, it was a relief to leave the bed when morning finally arrived, which set things rolling productively in order as I had decided. There was this grim determination in me, a kind of dark coldness that had taken me from rage to stifling my emotions. Sure, I was scared, but for the first time in three weeks, I felt I was in total control of the situation and my immediate environment. And with one last sweeping look at my room, I left the troubles and lamentations behind and walked out of the room with one thought – the good life had no place for a troubled soul. Each time our politicians falsified facts and stole billions; I see another brother get punished, while they walked proud and free. Despite the fact that I always viewed life as a wheel of fortune, and in my effort and desperation to spin it, I was hunted and hounded into a hole like a rat. But I'm done with that; I was no rat. I'm a black scorpion, and I sting hard!

More so, I was just a realer dying to make it in the harsh university environment; a place that had degenerated to a chaotic state, where life is brutish and short. An environment where academic scores are allocated to the highest bidder; a haven for sex workers and cultists; a place for future drugs dealers, fraudsters and armed robbers. It was obvious that I was the society's child – this was how they made me. I was done hiding and throwing myself a pity party. I headed to school and arrived just in time to join the meeting with the Dean and check my result before the end of session holidays began. Good thing, we had finished our exams before the Black Scorpion convention. Had we not, it would have been a different story for me.

****

During the holidays, I checked on Etete, and his family told me he was staying with his aunt, Ofege's mom, till after the holidays. Etete was still struggling badly with Ofege's death and needed time alone to process it all; for him, the best way of dealing with the loss was to spend time with Ofege's family in the home both of them had spent countless holidays as little boys. And Terror had travelled with his family to I-don't-know-where. So, I fell back on my old bosom peers, who were not so fortunate to get admitted into the university. In the evenings, we hooked up at a street corner discussing issues from the mundane to the inane. Girls were mostly the welcomed topic. Who slept with who? Who got pregnant, and who impregnated who?

I remember in one of our varied conversations, I had agreed to a bet with them about getting this new girl, Basirat, in our area to date me. We'd often made private jokes about her, calling her "mummy-rat" because of her name, and her robust size; she was very busty, dark-skinned, with full-rounded hips. So, I went all out to woo her, using some Yoruba words, which was the only language she spoke, but the Yoruba I had learnt was not enough to win this prized possession, and the English language was totally lost on her. So, in expressing my feelings for her one day, I held her wrist thinking she had finally succumbed to my proposals; she emptied the bucket of water she was carrying on me and thoroughly insulted me in the Yoruba language. The embarrassment was unquantifiable! I was drenched from head to toe; I felt like vanishing for the shame was too much to bear. As if that was not enough, she ran into a compound and continued to shout at me in her language. The scene was better described as a typical drama occasioned only when the hen lost her chicks to the kites; she raved and ranted, cursing my entire existence on earth. My friends could not help since it was an issue involving a weaker sex. I lost my rising profile, and my pride as someone who "belong" was badly dented by this girl. I lack the right adjectives to describe that encounter, and I also lost the courage to confront her again. In my private moment, I couldn't help but wonder if I would have tolerated this insolence from her if my Black Scorpion brothers were around; she most probably would have been dead by that same night. That made me realise how much I missed them and the adrenalin rush that being with them gave me.

By the third week of the holiday, life began to gather a bit of momentum in the town – since most students were not residents of Etinan, the university town's social life had gradually reduced. The populace was now beginning to adjust to a less busy street, and alcoholic joints were recording lower patronage. As dead as the town appeared to be, I noticed that some people were still making it big, spending and displaying so much money at will; their source of wealth was undoubtedly questionable. But it began to make sense why Capone used to love staying in Etinan during the long holidays – there was much room for money-making if one was smart. That triggered my Black Scorpion money-making senses, so, I decided it was time to make myself some money by all means possible as well. I became a thug for a few days because of the image of a "big boy" that I wanted to project and what the world was showing to me. My initial fear, mostly borne out of being alone without Black Scorpion members to back me, was banished.

The sun rose earlier than usual this morning, and the wind was chasing the cloud across the sky in the bright morning. While sitting by the window in our one-room house in a lonely compound, located on an isolated street, I noticed some secondary school students enter the compound, looking for no other person but me. Prior this, I had woken up hungry, thinking of what to eat as I had gone to bed having eaten only the small old *Afang* soup that had passed through several stove-warming for five days with an equally small mound of *Eba*. The attendant nightmares that followed ravaged what would have been a good night rest if I had eaten something better.

Before my visitors could get closer to our entrance door, I opened the door and acted like a tough guy. The tall one among them, who appeared to be their leader greeted me, displaying a weak smile. All of them joined with a chorus response when I responded to their leader's greetings. Then, their leader excused himself away from the others to dialogue with me alone as if the others were ignorant of the mission in the first instance. Now standing alone with me, he first ran his fingers across his well-trimmed, neat Afro-hair and scratched the corner of his right eye, where a small scar disappeared into the wrinkles of his smile; then, he shared their mission on why they needed to see me.

After narrating his story, it was evident that they needed somebody to "hit" their rival, Omang, who was a student at the University of Etinan. Going by his description, I could recall that there was a student like that I had seen in the Accounting Department. The mission piqued my interest, and I laid out my demands to him, which he agreed to meet, and the following couple of hours saw us trying to locate Omang's house. Every detail that would facilitate a "smooth and thorough beating" was made known to me. Omang was an average-height, dark-complexioned student in his early twenties; he was a bully with a knock-knee, always wearing goatee under a clean-shaven head. So dark was his skin that he had this perfect look of the Devil's first son. Since the image was familiar, we trekked to where he lived, which was a short distance away from the Mount Zion Bus Stop. While on our way, I moved with swag as if I, alone, would puncture the dignity of any tough boy in trouble with my payer; the truth be told, such a job required three to four hefty individuals to wreak serious havoc on Omang, who was not a *lepa* – skinny, like me. He was heavy-set like Sumo wrestler.

But splitting the little money with some of my old useless friends, who were still around was a wasteful idea to me, considering the financial state I was in. I thought that Omang would freeze when he learned that I was coming to deal with him, considering that my cult reputation preceded me. But he was not just my match; he became my superior as I came to him with neither weapon nor Black Scorpion hitmen. So, before I could bring him up to speed on the issue his four enemies had assigned to me, the bully held me by the neck, squeezing the living daylight out of me. He held on tight to my newly acquired T-shirt, which I saved money over a long period to buy. I struggled to free myself from his firm grip and attack, but a blow on my stomach from his left fist was enough to send me to the ground. I got up immediately and began throwing punches at him, but the blows were just hitting the air without making any impact. He charged forward at me, and another punch got me on my left eye, blinding me in the process while his missed upper-cut punch hit me on the right corner of my mouth. My tongue tasted something mildly salty; I knew it was blood. With my head spinning in pain, I wondered if I was here to beat or be beaten. For drawing blood, I leapt into the air to kick him, being the only Karate technique that I knew and remembered.

His two hands caught my leg, and a kick from him followed, and again, I was on the ground. Not giving me any chance to get up, he pinned me down with his massive frame, and what followed were brain-defying punches from all directions. When he was dragged off my body by a sympathiser, I thought the person who pulled him off my body

216

was one of those who had hired me. So, I called them to hold him down, and everybody would jointly beat him, but nobody responded. I wiped my face with my torn T-shirt before my vision became clear that my hirers had fled the scene, and Omang was still struggling to free himself from the man holding him back to devour me. Sensing danger, and a further round of onslaught, I tactically retreated because it would have been a total knock-out if he got his second chance at me.

When I got back home, I thanked God I survived. Most importantly, I got 5,000 Naira and two bottles of gin. At least, the money would sustain me for a while if effectively managed before the hard times drove in again. The news spread and my friends got wind of it and visited me. When they saw me, especially my face, they asked how many people beat me, leaving their mouths wide open. Trust me; I lied that it was a gang set-up. I suspected that they must have gotten the true picture of what had really happened, but I convinced them that I was set-up by a gang of boys. So, Omang and the four that hired me became our enemies and were placed on our local champ hit list. A glance at the mirror told the story: swollen eye, bleeding nose, and a cut on the lip. To simply sum it up; I was vandalised!

Though my old friends were planning for us to hit Omang, I had my own private plans underway for revenge. I strategised and prioritised, and every plan hinged on Etete's pocket and whatever was left of Black Scorpion upon school resumption. He, most likely, would be our first mission to announce we're back and stronger. My old friends never got around to helping me get my pound of flesh from Omang; I guess they were more scared of him than I imagined, but I was not worried, I still had my plans for him with the Black Scorpion.

The twelve-week long holidays finally came to an end, and school resumed for the first semester of the new session – my second year. Life was not really the same anymore. The fear associated with last semester killings and river deaths of tens of students pervaded the institution's landscape. The fears and rumours of reprisals were rife. I still had the off-campus apartment I shared with Etete but hadn't seen or spoken with him since the incident.

Now, I was not the type that could put any meaningful meal together; besides, it was not becoming of a true thug to cook. Cooking was not a great option for a growing "Hitman". So, I took to drinking and smoking as a way of assuaging my tension but messed up myself in the process, since I had no partner in crime like Etete or Terror or Ofege or Undertaker to have my back in the common event of stupidity from drunkenness. Thus, I became an object of amusement before fellow students living around my off-campus apartment premises – coming back home without a properly buttoned shirt or it would be hanging open on my shoulder, with a loosened belt buckle, and sometimes, without one of my shoes, walking with one foot bare. It was a ridiculous fashion, and I was a terrible sight, to say the least. I stank like a wrong blend of chemicals in a science lab, with a repulsive breath. And in less than one week of school resumption, I was back to "square one" – in want and lack.

After two days, Terror entered the campus, surprising everybody against his earlier plans of returning late. I happened to know this from a note he had dropped inside a letterbox beside my door. Two hours later, I was at his house, but the roaming guy was not there. So, as usual, I also dropped a note scheduling how we should meet. Since we normally meet in such circumstance at an alcoholic joint, on an adjoining street close to the school's main entrance, I strolled down there with the hope of seeing the man behind many skirmishes in our clique, and I could not locate him even at this most likely place. However, I did not give up hope of seeing him since I knew that seeing him would guarantee me some money or food. After exploring all avenues, and our likely fun spots to no avail, I returned to my place, knowing that as an old informinua, he would be ready to meet me to brief me or get briefed, whichever came first.

CHAPTER THIRTEEN

Etete finally returned to school two weeks after the resumption. I had already left for the campus when he arrived at our apartment, so, showed up with Terror to see me at my department. We were both overjoyed to see each, hugging, loud handshakes, talking and making so much noise, not caring that lectures were going on in some classrooms. We finally parted with plans to meet up after our last lectures and return to the apartment together to catch up. The day was dragging too slow, and lectures seemed to be taking forever to end. I was just like a little boy with a new toy, too excited and couldn't wait for my lectures to be over to see my guys.

That afternoon at the apartment with Etete and Terror, the long-awaited information finally came.

Nsa, in a rush on duty, as usual, and without formalities, announced the meeting had been scheduled for 11:30pm tonight at the usual place in the thick forest. The meeting would also be an initiation ceremony for some members into their new roles in higher positions. It was not easy forgetting Udofia; his death was a significant loss to our organisation. I remember last semester, immediately after we got back to school from the non-convention, we had all gone to his two apartments to evacuate his Black Scorpion properties before his parents arrived, Etim Nkanta took hold of his Capone regalia and whispered into my ears that he was the next Capone, urging me to stand by him. The information sank into my brain, but I was completely indifferent to his lobbying.

However, we couldn't effectively function without a Capone. There was a noticeable division among high-ranking members of our group. Each favoured another for the position of the Capone. Everybody with any vital position in the organisation was acting like the Capone; everyone wanted to control others. Sometimes, orders were rebuffed or rejected simply because it didn't emanate from a recognised sitting Capone. A typical scenario was an order from the Bossman for every member to get the scorpion tattoo at an agreed location; that day, only eight members turned up, including me. Another leading member called for a meeting to prepare for an attack against one of our rivals; not a single soul showed up for the hit.

It was obvious that we were heading towards disintegration as there was no central command. During that period, Chief Nyong, Etete's father, escaped assassination and suspected cultists were blamed for the attempt on his life. Etete soon realized that his father was becoming a target by our rivals and spoke up about it, but nobody did anything about it. Many in the political circle simply assumed and dismissed these assassination attempts as the usual scenario whenever election draws near in the state. That same week, four days after Etete's father, Etim Nkanta's paternal uncle, whom Black Scorpion had been protecting, was assassinated; the footprint bore the mark of one of our rivals. That was when we realised that our activities had become an open secret to our rivals; they were always accurately a step ahead of us – Black Scorpion had become sheep without a shepherd, therefore, free for the wolves to devour, yet all eyes remained on us. So, since most of us were becoming known to the school authority, we decided to fly under the radar; most of our activities became more concealed, or worse still, almost non-existent for lack of a leader.

Many of the members clamoured for the Zonal Butcher, Boma's right-hand man, Belema, whose family was extremely rich and influential, to become Capone, despite knowing the standard order of the system; it had to be the next in line after the Capone – the Bossman. But they didn't care about that, and also that Belema had a foul temperament and could kill his own member without a thought; all that mattered was the wealth and influence behind him. I never really liked the Zonal Butcher; aside from the punishment he gave me at the river during the ill-fated convention that saved my life, his death did not bother me. Also, I disliked his temperament and sense of judgment, which was much like Belema's. But the competition seemed set between these two. So, having Etim Nkanta, the Bossman was what I looked forward to; he was the only option for me.

After much ado about nothing, Etim Nkanta was chosen according to the Black Scorpion standards by the organisation's Zonal Godfather, understanding that we can't effectively coordinate the organisation without a Capone. Thus, the date was set for his swearing-in as the new Capone tonight. Leaving nothing to chance, when we all arrived the venue at 11.15pm, the venue was changed; we stealthily scaled the cemetery fence and moved far away from the forest we all had in mind for the meeting. We accessed the burial ground and walked further down to somewhere in the thicket and hid for about ten minutes. After we had ascertained the coast was clear of any rivals or security agents, we quickened our steps to another thicket closer to a tree. As usual, bags containing our arsenal were opened, and three of our hitmen stood sentry against any intruder. The rest of us proceeded to arrange certain materials for the swearing-in of the Capone. There were black and red pieces of clothing materials, rings, two daggers with red pieces of cloth tied to each and red candles. Others were two bottles of *Ufofop* - a local brew.

The Black Scorpion Zonal Godfather was present for the initiation of the cult's new Capone. He was dressed like the devil in all black and stood tall beyond comprehension with his face partially concealed, and Etim Nkanta stood beside him in hooded-skeleton regalia looking like death itself. The regalia was of black clothing, and cowries adorned it; a skull symbol was on the back of the hood while in front, the chest had the Black Scorpion symbol as the heart of the skeleton adorning the front and back of the regalia. It's said that the regalia was fortified – capable of shielding bullets. They were both lost in a deep conversation with each other, and there was dead silence amongst us; no one moved or talked, unlike our usual meetings punctuated with much noise, smoking, and drinking.

Suddenly they both raised their heads as if just noticing the rest of us, and in a loud voice, Etim Nkanta called out three names – Terror, Etete and I, and asked us to come forward and stand beside him, which we did. The Zonal Godfather stepped out to stand before the four of us, touching our shoulders with something that looked like a red or bloody machete; his face was still partially concealed; we could only see his eyes, which looked hollow and mean. I was the last person he touched with the machete, after which he turned around, facing the other members and lifted his hands and laughed out loud.

"These are the chosen ones. Let the ceremony begin!" He announced in an eerily loud, deep voice.

Nsa lit one of the red candles which helped in illuminating the tombstone, but the breeze was gathering speed, extinguishing it time and again. Soon it started to drizzle, and I began to shiver. Etim Nkanta was brought forward; he had smoked his mixture to a climax. He started making funny sounds like the howls of a hyena, leaping into the air in an apparent depiction of Ibibio nation warrior dance. He would surge forward with fiery blazing eyeballs, then retreat and do it all over again. And at that same time, midnight came falling, and the night activities kicked off; we choreographed the night's caper with the Chief Sailor, Tekena Peters, leading the songs with his Songitos. Then, we carried on our longstanding tradition of the blood oath, and the bow of acceptance: the natural reaction of all members to the cult's higher power that concealed itself within the cloak of secrecy. And for me, it was a culmination of my own quest for power and significance, one that had become personalised since experiencing affluence with Etete.

Meanwhile, the Zonal Godfather was mixing some I-don't-know-what concoction. A few minutes later, the rain finally came down, and we were drenched from head to toe. The Leader called for the oath-taking of Etim Nkanta to formalise his Caponeship. Etim was still moving in wild gyration like an Ekpo masquerade on an errand. Then something was sprinkled on him, and he became impulsively sober, though, he quivered intermittently with his face mottled in the dark, glaring balefully at us. In the ensuing frightful developments, I became afraid, then the Zonal Godfather murmured incantations and there descended a creepy silence. The only sound was the whistling of the breeze and droplets of rain.

Etim Nkanta was instructed to sit on the tombstone, and the oath-taking began. A calabash containing cowries and Guinea Fowl eggs was given to him, his blood was collected as usual by tapping him on the wrist with a sharp knife. After this, the Zonal Godfather performed yet another blood oath – a special "leaders' blood oath", which included Etete, Terror and me, drawing blood himself with a short, sharp knife from each of our upper thighs, and Nsa collected each one's blood in a skull-shaped glass cup bearing the image of a black scorpion, after which the Zonal Godfather poured in some gin, along with some powder and mixed it, offering each of us to take a sip and also drank some himself. Another round of incarnation followed. To fortify the new Capone, a human skull was brought forward; the skull was used to circle his head thrice as he repeated the incantations from the Zonal Godfather. Then he was given some seeds to chew, and as he chewed, I perceived the scent of alligator pepper; then sap from leaves was squeezed into his mouth, palm fronds were tied around his neck, hands and legs.

At last, the initiation of the Black Scorpion new leaders was completed – it was 3.15am. Etim Nkanta became our Capone, taking over from Udofia who died at the river. Terror was sworn in as the new Bossman; Etete as the Lead Hitman, and I, having shed more blood than Etete, according to the Zonal Godfather, proved myself a formidable force, was initiated as the Zonal Butcher – the Undertaker, taking over from Boma, who also died at the river. A red-hot seal bearing a black scorpion's image was pulled out of the blazing fire and stamped on Capone's left shoulder; he did not even as little as wince; I wondered if he was really human or just metal with acid running inside him. The rest of the leaders did not get the seal; it was only for the Capone.

By this time, cold from the rain had intensified, and

we were all shivering like day-old chicks. Hurriedly, materials used for the initiation were bagged, and we sneaked out of the cemetery. On our way home, police officers on patrol in a Hilux truck noticed our suspicious movements and chased after us. We fled unto an uneven road, and within a few seconds, the headlight of the Hilux truck was beaming at us. I dashed into a bush and made for the fence before me. Just then, I heard a gunshot; I slipped and fell from the slippery fence out of fright. The bullet hit the Zonal Godfather on his right leg; he had veered into the bush in an obvious attempt to follow me. Looking around first to ensure the officers were not in sight, I got up and moved to his spot to help him. His black Jean trouser was beginning to soak up with blood and water from the rain. Despite urging him to bear it and try to move faster, leaping seemed to be the only form of movement he could muster, and we needed more than that to escape arrest by the police. Thus, knowing that waiting to assist him could spell doom for me, I dashed towards the fence again and made it safely to the apartment, where Etete and Terror were already waiting.

Later that morning, at about 10:15am, we got news that the Zonal Godfather was not captured by the police and was receiving treatment privately at his house. Capone was safe, and most of the members got to their abodes safely. Only two members were arrested, and Capone was already working on getting them released. I was too tired with a blinding headache to attend lectures, so, I stayed back in the apartment, sleeping most of the day and only woke up to eat when one of the female members, Adiaba, brought me some food. Etete was up and about with Terror on some business dealings in town.

The following day, I walked to campus with Etete for lectures like most other school days; everything was going smoothly, nothing appeared unusual. I had walked this campus for over a year now, so, I know the bad guys just the same as if they were etched in my head with a sharp knife, scored in deep like some strange work of art. These same routes, I had walked with my guys, and for the most part, I was calm here, at least in the morning or afternoon, with a steady heartbeat. And this day didn't seem any different; there were no warning signs of danger as I finished my last class at about 2:45pm to join Etete, who was waiting for me outside. My senses were on zero alerts; the sun was even calmer, and the breeze was cooler. The day was so easy, I did not even think or say, as usual, my all-time favourite words from my grandpa's wisdom that until the head of any serpent is removed, you ignore the body at your own peril; maybe the words would have alerted me of impending danger. Nothing was unusual enough to spike my adrenaline; every stranger was friendly. Yet, they were all-around us marking out their turf like a wolf pack, and we did not even notice.

"Be wary of friendly gestures from strange fellows". This was one of the rules of survival when you "belong" to organisations such as ours. But this day, none of us took cognisance of that rule. A certain student had approached three of us – Etete, Terror and I, on our way back to the apartment after lectures. After the customary handshake, this student, seemingly new, was about to ask us for directions, at least so we thought, when another student, out of nowhere, bumped into the four of us standing, with Etete being the worst hit, and thus, fell to the ground. Then, yet another student ran forward and apologised, parking up our books and files that had scattered all over the ground. A few other students around joined in and expressed heartfelt concern for Etete, touching him to ascertain he was not badly impacted. Soon enough, many other students gathered around us in a show of sympathy. This left us with no suspicion at all, believing the bump into us was a mere accident; thus, our guards were down.

I reached down to help Etete back up on his feet, and while he was still dusting off his jeans trouser, we heard a gunshot in our midst, which sent many students fleeing for their lives, including Terror and me. When I was a safe distance away and realising Etete was neither behind nor beside me, the bond of friendship made me stop and turn to look at the spot where the student had bumped into us; I saw Etete being led away by the same students that showed affection for him when he was knocked down. I did not see Terror; he'd outran me, so I had no idea which way he had gone.

About four students held him on his Jeans trousers, while others were brandishing dangerous weapons, looking around for anyone who would dare come close. The guys taking him away moved like a multi-headed beast that shared only one brain. Their thoughts were in lockstep as much as their feet; their mood swirled in mean currents beneath the dark surface of their faces. I became really scared and worried as I felt Etete would soon be a dead man. Helplessly, I moved away from the place

I stood for safety and to get a perfect view of my friend's last moments, as I thought it would be. Another gunshot was fired into the air to disperse all other students, but my new hideout was a spot I needed in this kind of situation, so I remained there.

There was no form of resistance from Etete, except only rubbing his hands together; I guess pleading to be spared. One of them handed another a rope, as yet another kicked Etete down; he was tied up with the rope, from his left upper arm to his legs and pushed down flat on the ground, leaving the right arm free and spread out. Within a twinkle of an eye, one of the student assailants swung down a machete at him, which stabbed him on the right wrist. Etete let out a sharp cry and sprang up to flee but was held down by three strong men. One of the students jumped on his back and grabbed the bleeding hand. Another student held his two legs together while the student with the machete gave him repeated blows with the machete on the same bleeding wrist. On the fourth blow, Etete's right wrist was severed from his hand; he shouted in agony and leapt back and forth, yelping, when he was untied and set free. No soul responded until his attackers fled the scene with his dismembered wrist.

A female student braved it to Etete's rescue, but she could not do much. Another help came to the scene and screamed for help. I could not volunteer to help as such assistance might be dangerous. I fled the scene when I was sure that some students were assisting him, and the university hospital's ambulance was on its way. My cowardly mind reasoned away my actions, convincing me that if I was the one, none of our guys would risk their lives for mine – at least not immediately while the attacking group may still be lurking around for more blood. No; they would show up when the coast was clear, and then retaliate later. But I knew I was lying to myself; Etete would risk his life for me, and he'd proven that a few times, even at the river. Battling with my conscience, I reminded myself that the organisation's code was to save yourself first, and "we" retaliate later. Still, I felt like a coward and heartbroken that I could not be there to help my friend; tears of shame and pain rolled down my face as I heard the siren from the ambulance when it drove away with him.

It turned out that Etete had been on our rival cult's surveillance note, and their "hit list". None of us knew until that afternoon. His own predicament was termed as an inappropriate association with the wrong company. Being from a wealthy family, coupled with his fine, friendly, innocent appearance, the kind of friends that flocked around him was the one issue that bothered and bored everybody because with him, we couldn't tell friend from foe; anyone could walk up to Etete for a friendly chat, which made it difficult to get suspicious about anyone walking up to him. His friends were, perhaps, too many for his own good. But one thing was certain: he was rich and popular, which was the magnet that attracted all manner of unwholesome individuals to him. His unfortunate attack was a warning by his attackers to us.

The news of the incident had reached every nook and cranny of the campus and beyond. That night, members of our organisation hurriedly assembled and protested in the known language of the cult – gunshots. There was no movement of any kind at night as several gunshots were being fired randomly. The institution's security apparatus was laid bare; those old retired cowards or soldiers or whatever they called themselves, who claimed "not tired" were not our match in terms of firepower. These security men, who barely fed well, would not risk their miserable lives for our course, nor waste their numbered bullets; they were all retired soldiers from both the Nigerian and the defunct Biafran army.

The Black Scorpions unleashed unimaginable terror on the campus that night; we were revered next, after God. Many innocent students were injured, and some of the female students were gang raped. Windshields of parked cars got most of the brutality; three department signposts were pulled down at the generating house that supplied power to the university community in the event of power outage from the ever-failing public supply system. Two of the generating plants were set ablaze. A Student Union Government bus was vandalised, while the Nigeria national flag of green-white-green, which was already a rag in the air, was lowered and torn into shreds.

In my rage that same night, I told Terror how Omang had me set up and badly beaten during the holidays insinuating that he may have something to do with Etete's ordeal, although we knew Omang didn't belong to any cult; he was a one-man warrior. So, we sought him out. He didn't see us coming in the darkness, until it was too late, and my hand had connected with his jaw, giving him a perfect taste of my signature move designed to incapacitate my victim – a sharp uppercut that almost had him cleave his tongue in half with his own teeth; the impact was mind-bending. While he was still trying to find his bearings, groaning and holding his bleeding mouth, I said, "Now, that's for the blood you drew from me, and the rest is to show you who's in charge in Etinan."

Then, Terror and I descended on him, beating, punching and kicking him with all the rage in us until he had no more strength left even to cry or beg for his life. We left him bleeding all over, but alive. And then, we continued on our main mission to join Capone in seeking out the real perpetrators of the dastardly act against Etete.

By dawn, three students from the rival fraternity were reportedly killed. This was to be pacification for the unprovoked attack on Etete and a warning to any other rival group. But I was still inconsolable, filled with anger and sadness at Etete's horrifying ordeal – the pain I watched him go through was unbearable. After all that rain of violence, I lay curled up in a friend's bed in the male hostel without venturing outside, except to the bathroom. Troops from the Nigeria Police Force had invaded our campus, along with the Military and halted every other activity. Some popular students and members of the Student Union executives were apprehended. Majority of them were innocent, of course.

The following day, I went to check on Etete at the university clinic and found that he had been moved to one of the private clinics in the city. As expected, I visited him there and met their domestic servant by his bedside; he was fast asleep, and his dark oval face had the look of an angel. Some of the statements extracted from Etete had me in most of his programmes on that day. This led to more arrests, including some members of our organisation, but I was the most wanted man of all. During my last visit to Etete at the hospital, I had explained to him about my inability to stand by him that day, and my financial state if I was eventually arrested. So, he carefully re-christened me to evade arrest for me, claiming he was disoriented being heavily drugged with pain medications, and so got the name wrong. And Onofiok became my new name in the report, but he couldn't change my description that he gave them.

On several occasions, the Black Scorpion members' off-campus apartments and campus rooms were ransacked and searched for arms by the police to use as evidence, which yielded no results – nothing was found. However, it was suspected that I was a member as they believed that my bosom friend, Etete, was a member, or he wouldn't have been singled out as a target. I neither accepted, defended, nor denied any of their speculations; besides my name is Aniete, not Onofiok, so there was really nothing to defend. Etete also did none of the above; we're not snitches. Besides, we know the price of snitching; it's worse than what the law could do to us.

It was difficult to shake off the toga of cultism, be it Anietie or Onofiok. And that called for a new identity; thus, my bald, skin-cut head, which was the prominent and notable fashion amongst the males in the system had to give way to a more friendly haircut, at least for a change. And I started wearing some over-sized, old-fashioned Jeans trousers from Etete's house and any T-shirt most of the time after school. I also disguised myself to have a clean-shaven look – no more *goatee* beards, which I used to keep. My final disguise was to always wear to class, "cut and sew" black trouser and shirt with a cheap bowtie and round ugly unmedicated glasses, looking like a nerd.

In the evenings, I would stroll under cover of darkness to any crowded Church to attend their evening service; I did these for almost 14 days. The constant lucid nightmares broke my indomitable spirit. During these days in the wilderness, I saw the hypocrisy of some Christian denominations. In one orthodox denomination I attended, graven images from paintings, sculptures and drawings hung within and outside the Church premises. Most prominent were that of a certain bearded man from the Caucasian race in his early thirties as the images depicted, in different moods, stretching his hands towards children: People going into the Church would kneel and bow before these images. At intervals, during the service, some songs were rendered in foreign language, which I guessed should be somewhere from Europe. Many praises were rendered to the mother of the Saviour than the Saviour Himself. This happened on the first day of my religious sojourn to the house of God.

The following day was the training of choristers in that Church; so, I chose another denomination adjoining my off-campus apartment street. It seemed these days Churches were everywhere with all kinds of names and miraculous claims. Since a known friend worshipped there, I considered it a good place to seek God at this dark period of my life. Immediately I stepped into the Church auditorium, I heard shouts of fire, fire, fire! Initially, my mind went to the Pentecost days in the epoch of the apostle. Bewildered as I was, I thought the worshippers would ascend into heaven, but that did not happen; instead, every member was shaking violently and still chanting fire. Soon, I realised that I was also calling for fire in a shameful small voice. Among the sparse crowd was my friend, Kofi, speaking different languages periodically, and this is a Ghanaian, who only spoke English and Ashanti. And there he was speaking in a foreign language, and also shouting fire. I guessed his act indicated speaking in tongues. I was amazed that at the ring of a bell, all of them would become quiet no matter how divinely obsessed they were; an "ordinary" hand-held bell always calmed them. Well, maybe the bell wasn't an ordinary one.

At the end of it all, nothing much was ministered but occasional quotes from the Bible. And of course, prayers for fire to consume anything evil from wall geckoes to human beings, and the rest of the world. That night, I thought the service would never end; many prayers were offered for all kinds of ailment and diseases, and fire seemed to be the famed factor needed to conquer these infirmities. If their miraculous claims were to be substantiated, my bleeding heart goes to the health workers and aspiring ones, for very soon they would be out of jobs. While this was going on though, the fire could not consume the deserving NEPA officials, who were on duty at a station and responsible for the "wicked act" of blackout experienced throughout the service.

A few minutes before 9:00pm, I left before they could get a chance to call for new members to step forward. On their signpost, I saw what appeared to be fire on top of the hill or a mountain, and I thought; perhaps, a fire station should be built nearby just in case fire engulfed them from this unending chant of fire.

The next evening in another Church. This time, it was a denomination that claimed to derive their inspirations from the manners of the apostles. Using drums and heavy percussion, wild dancing was matched with wild singing in the indigenous language. Latest seductive dance steps that we were practising in the clubs were displayed with ease here. Wriggling the waist by women was a delightful sight to behold, but to me, a sight so disdainful for a Christ-seeking sinner like me. To them, the Lord was always good, to which they chorused – "all the time".

Thus, I went from denomination to denomination each evening. The one that surpassed them all was the one that the man at the podium used all kinds of gimmicks to demand money from the poverty-stricken members. He seemed to be the only well-fed and well-clothed individual amongst the few before me. Building appeal fund was demanded, money for the Church secondary school and university scholarship project, Church logo launching, offerings, tithes, Church upkeep, and of course, he then advised members to still sow a financial seed for their personal success upon all of these.

"God loves a cheerful giver," he announced excitedly, "give so that God will replenish you in good measure, shaken together and running over," he cheered on, quoting all known verses that had to do with emptying one's purse and pocket.

"This is a BUSINESS CENTRE!" I thoughtfully concluded.

The smartly dressed young pastor spoke impeccable English throughout the evening sermon. He must have been one of those out-of-job-graduates, who were now gainfully employed in the ministry. He said God called him, but I have my doubts; I think he was the one that actually called God.

This was it for me: my mind was made up to stop or possibly change to an entirely new faith, but I was not ready to learn Arabic in old age and be washing my hands, legs and face whenever I wanted to commune with my Creator. From my perspective, it seemed that in Islam, God only understands one language – Arabic, and also, without water, you cannot call unto Him. Then again, it did not help that my fears were further fanned by the many violent activities of its adherents in the northern parts of Nigeria and the Middle East. Many extremists worse than us in Black Scorpion found solace and breeding ground in this religion. So, as the good coward that I was, I threw in the towel amidst a good fight of faiths. Then, experiencing the different facets of the other side, I found it was really difficult for me to assimilate the doctrine of one God but different denominations; or better still, one God and a different mode of worship. I guess anything else outside of these was preferable. I tried.

CHAPTER FOURTEEN

The police hunt for the cult members that unleashed the deadliest killings in the university was still on, and even more desperate now with me on the MOST WANTED list. The rival cult members arrested had given up my name to the powers that be. It so happened that these killings had directly touched the heart of the powers that be: Two of the Governor's relatives had been killed – his only son, who belonged to the rival cult and his nephew. Capone, Terror and I captured both of them along with their Capone, and I specifically pulled the trigger at the Governor's son, shooting him point-blank on the forehead, and then, put a bullet at close range on each of his wrists, shattering the bones and veins. I was filled with venom when I learnt he was the mastermind of the horrifying hit on Etete based on a dispute his father had had with Etete's father, which negatively affected his father's chances of re-elections with their party members. The attack was completely uncalled for, and to take away Etete's right hand, which he wrote his tests, exams, signatures, and any good work for his future, was simply unforgivable! So, I needed to do the honours of taking him out personally for my friend and to assuage my guilt of having abandoned him at the hit scene. I shot his wrists as a reminder to his group of their unprovoked violence against a young man, who was still recuperating in hospital. A young man who would never again use his natural fingers because they took it away and ensured the wrist died to destroy any slim chance that the wrist might be attached back to his hand.

Since my "Christian brother" disguise had proved more frustrating than good, I moved home to my grandpa's house, out of Etinan, to lay low and stay in hiding, without Grandpa's knowledge. That evening, I sneaked into the storehouse at Grandpa's, then slipped into my underwear and curled up on the mat that had been there for ages, whose only coverage was an old rag towel that has seen more years than its owner. Interestingly, the darkness in the room provided a befitting cover for such circumstance. I folded my left hand to form an angular pillow for my head, but sleep evaded me like a plague, and I stared into the blankness that has become my world.

Later that night, around 9:00pm, two vehicles screeched at the entrance of our compound, and my head jerked into consciousness. Footsteps began to march into the compound with ferocity. My aged grandfather, who always made the front of the store I was hiding in "a breeze taking spot", hollered at the approaching figures in the darkness with a weak voice, "Who is that?"

His second attempt at the same question was accompanied by a chesty cough, followed by a groan, and then some murmurings that were not audible from my spot.

"We're looking for Anietie Akpabio," one of the officers said.

"The young man you people are looking for is my grandson; he's at school. Is all well?" Grandpa asked pleadingly.

"Search the whole building," one of the policemen said.

"Please, my children," Grandpa begged, "let no harm come his way if you see him. Spare his young life and bring him to me, please."

"Papa! Your grandson is a criminal, and he is wanted."

"That cannot be; I raised him. His father, who was my son, was snatched by the cold hands of death some years ago, leaving him to my care," he responded, almost counting the words, "so, please, spare me another agony-,"

"Papa! *If your grandson dey around, tell-am make him come out, make him surrender...o,*" one of the policemen said in pidgin, interrupting him before he could finish his sentences.

Suddenly, the policeman who was speaking with Grandpa corked his rifle. I heard my grandfather trying to get up from his seat; the old chair creaked as usual without ever breaking.

"Spare me another grief," I heard him as he tried to follow the policemen.

They entered every room in the compound, searching earnestly for me. I could also hear our other relatives, exchanging words with the policemen each time they threatened to shoot if I was not produced. But none of them could hand me to them, since none had neither seen me nor knew that I was within the premises.

Since I was not seen, trust our policemen to get

creative; they arrested every young man in sight to swell their bail purse. Some of the police officers came out with choice electronics and phones, demanding the receipts from their owners or they should consider them confiscated as stolen items. The police were quite good with the law when it's tilted in their favour. I could not understand the degree of greed that had become the lot of our uniformed men. Everything was an exhibit. Still, the people were told to remain silent as whatever they said would be used as evidence in the law court against them. But I do know that silence in law here meant acceptance and or connivance with whatever they did to the culprits. So, how then does an individual get free from these entire legal shenanigans? What then was the difference between a madman and policeman? Filthy corrupt killers! And they dare to accuse and arrest me for what was a lifestyle for them! Bloody Hypocrites!

Immediately the police left with their loot, I tip-toed into the room that served as my grandpa's room, fully dressed, as if I had just arrived at the house and whispered a greeting to him. But the muteness of the old man suggested something different to me. My dear grandpa, whose fate had turned him into fathering me, was looking gaunt, dishevelled and lost; he must have been shocked into silence by the police gunshots outside. He neither heard nor saw me, and I did not touch him so as not to startle him further into a heart attack. Looking at his chest, I saw he was breathing, so I left him to come out of the shock on his own.

I looked ruffled though, when I came out of the storehouse; cobwebs ran riot all over my body; dust and fetid smell of old clothes ravaged my breath. I would have been caught save for some benevolent spirit that showed the cops a greedy escape route, which they happily followed. Moments later, I heard my relatives slaughtering my character into bits and pieces; I did not want to blame them or argue issues with them. Nobody saw my struggles to get a decent education, but they're all quick to see my troubles, especially Aniema's mother, my father's elder sister, who was having a field day vomiting her biases against me. I could only attribute her vituperations as the ranting of an ant, and the pains of her unmarried status and the unprofitable business venture she engaged in. She claimed to be a seller of assorted items but a close look at her wares, one would realise that she sold assorted rubbish.

That day, listening to my relatives, I realised that love was an orphan, whose eventual funeral had no attendant. I was murdered long ago by this same paternal family judging me today, when they took everything from my mother and her young children, leaving us hungry and begging for what was rightfully ours. This provocative thought brought more pain to my already troubled soul; my agony was multiplied. The same demon I thought that I had long conquered raised its ugly head once again to devour me; thus, again, I became a prisoner of conscience, tossed to and fro life's rough waves; I became a slave without a master. The tenacity to respond to their ranting was not in me as escape was a wealthier and healthier option for me to explore.

I crept back to the old storehouse and shifted the ceiling board to hide; the floor was no longer safe. Sleep evaded me while I hung in-between the roofing beams like a roasted chicken. Sleep eventually came, but a few minutes later, I was woken up by a loud banging on the storehouse door. Within a twinkle of an eye, the policemen broke down the door, and four of them stepped inside. Their shouting rented the air; they threatened to shoot, despite not finding me inside. Everything, including outdated items that could possibly hide a human being, was searched and scattered. Their effort, however, yielded dividend when a stupid rat chased another rat towards my direction. As the rodents climbed my back, the phobia I had for such creatures made me shift, and with that movement, I made a sound with the ceiling board, which gave me out.

"God punish that rat!" I cursed under my breath.

This added more dimension for the police as they shot twice into a different direction in the ceiling, ordering whosoever that was hiding there to come out. I climbed down to avoid being hit by the bullets. It was amazing to find that the police numbered over a dozen just to arrest one human – me. I was dragged at the waist by the jeans trousers I wore. Sporadic gunshots were fired into the air outside after they already had me in their custody – what a waste of government resources. Some of these cowards began to jubilate at apprehending a common civilian like me, a young man of barely twenty-one years. Even in the darkness, I could see that smiles lined up their suffering faces, celebrating my capture when they could not withstand the firepower of armed bandits. People came out, mostly those who were going for early morning Mass at the Catholic Church nearby. I realised then that it was just a few minutes before five; little wonder the huge Church bell was not rung. It could also mean that the police had laid siege for me two hours earlier. And thinking about it now, the police seemed so sure that I was inside that storehouse; I bet one of my arrested relatives' parents must have seen me when I sneaked back in there and leaked my hideout to the police.

As I walked to the police Hilux truck, I felt a certain relief wash over me; my mind could no longer play tricks on me. The looming shadows of death from rival cult groups vanished as I felt that in police custody, I would not be reached or touched by those ruthless agents of death. And looking around me as I walked past the early risers, I saw eyes that were surprised that I was arrested for cult activities, and some who doubted my involvement – their tear-filled eyes told the story, while others stood in mockery, saying, "YES! YOU HAVE BEEN CAUGHT." All eyes remained trained on me as the police handcuffed me to an upright metal bar at the open back of the old, rickety Hilux truck. Tears of frustration welled up in my eyes, and I let it roll down my face, not for me but for what I had done to my grandpa, leading this people to his own domain to witness this public walk of shame from a place he had held so dear and called home all his life. But as the truck pulled away, I wiped my tears and smiled; I felt sure that Capone and the Black Scorpions would get me out soon, as always, and I would make it all right for Grandpa.

Sunday dawned bright and quiet, and I laid on the bare, hard floor listening to my thoughts in the quietness of the cell at the Etinan Police Station, but about a couple of hours later, we heard raucous chorused greetings from the policemen at the counter. Looking through the metal bars, I noticed that a superior officer had arrived at the premises. The DPO of the station sauntered into the dirty front office like a prince from the harmattan region. He looked so weary and tired from exhaustion.

"Good morning, sir," a Sergeant saluted when the DPO approached him.

"What's good about the morning?" The DPO retorted.

"All correct, sir," he saluted again, with the terminology used to concur and cooperate with corrupt acts and intentions.

The other three junior officers responded in unison in their ever-willing corrupt manner.

"Everybody, assemble here, now!" The DPO

commanded, and five other footsteps hurriedly raced into the front office and stood at attention.

The DPO quickly told them to stand at ease. "I have information for all of you," he thundered; hand akimbo like a harbinger of misfortune to the underpaid junior officers.

"We're all at your service, sir," one of the wretched -looking officers replied, saluting again.

In my perturbed mind, I had thought that corruption would soon be a thing of the past as was promised by successive government and its various anti-corruption agencies. Unknown to me, there was a whole different dimension to it with our police officers because the next words that the DPO vomited shocked me to the marrow.

"I've just lost my mother, boys," the DPO announced, pausing to observe their reaction before continuing, "so, I'll need over N80,000 (Naira) for a befitting state burial, worthy of a queen, for her. This is the amount I want from you all before the end of the month; the burial will be coming up in less than two months. I need to start making some payments before then."

"Consider it done, sir," they chorused like kindergarten pupils.

"Thank you, boys," the DPO answered and turned to leave.

"But excuse me, sir," a thin voice called out, stopping the DPO.

"Yes; go on Constable," the DPO said in anticipation.

"Sir, all our Patrol vehicles are grounded," the Constable said, "the white Hilux truck being the only one working, is without fuel."

"Look for the money and fuel that," the DPO said, "you do not need to tell me that. Do you want me to donate my blood for your patrol tonight?" He thundered.

With that the junior officers ran helter-skelter, searching through different files that could yield an immediate financial result for fuel, while the DPO waited; they found one with a pending case of rape, which was reviewed immediately. The suspect, a young man in his early twenties, was told to add the sum of five thousand Naira to the earlier "demanded" twenty thousand, which his elder brother already came with and was waiting for someone to attend to him. Since there was no additional money on him to add as the police officer demanded, the DPO, feigning grounds of compassion and leniency, instructed the Sergeant to collect the twenty thousand Naira that he brought to pay. A photocopied paper was presented to the suspect's elder brother to append his signature.

Immediately after the DPO left, I saw their patrol vehicle being pushed out of the premises by the officers, the suspect and his elder brother. Three and half hours after that, nine males and one female were arrested and brought back to the station by these police officers for various fictitious offences. As the police emptied them into one of the unoccupied cells, the arrested individuals were reminded of their offences and advised to bail themselves with the sum of ten thousand naira each. However, if they didn't pay immediately, there would be an increment each day they miss the payment. A few of them that had money on them begged and paid their way to freedom, while those of them without money made the stinking cell their abode for the night, despite their pleas and claims of innocence.

At the end of the unofficial extortion, the sum of twenty thousand Naira was collected from two of the three young adult males. The last was later released with the sum of three thousand Naira, being the only money on him, and also claiming that nobody would come for his bail since he was just a traveller passing through the state. He was set free after about 45 minutes delay with a few slaps and insults for being too poor to pay ten thousand. An hour later, a vehicle screeched to a halt outside the police station. As I thought, and eventually confirmed, the police had made yet another set of arrests. A group of young men were ushered into the police station. Some were in handcuffs, while others had both hands tied together with a piece of clothing, which I believe were their shirts.

The young men were charged for wandering at night – it was only 7:30pm, and also for resisting arrest when law enforcement agents accosted them. A female victim among them was crying throughout the "harassment" process. She was later cuddled to stop crying and taken outside in the prevailing darkness by one of the officers. After a while, her cry diminished and was replaced with soft moans of pleasure, and maybe, pain.

"Useless animals," I retorted, forgetting where I was for a second.

I was snapped back to reality by approaching footsteps of two individuals walking toward the cells. When they began to whisper, I knew instantly that it was the traumatised girl and her forced policeman lover. Two benches were arranged together to form a wooden bed for her comfort, and she lay still. At that point, I simply decided to mind my own business, and sleep took control of me until the first light of Monday morning appeared.

Around 9:00am on Monday morning when we were called out to give the police officer on duty our addresses and contact persons for our bail, there was no trace of the girl anywhere there. While on the wall inside the front office was boldly written "BAIL IS FREE", we were charged several large sums of money; mine was particularly much – fifty thousand Naira. It would appear only the girl was released free; well, of course, she already paid in kind, and probably, to more than one police officer through the night. Many of the arrested victims were released only after their relatives had met the "officers-generated" bail conditions. Through a rough estimation, a total of one hundred thousand and above went into the policemen pockets, within twenty-four hours timeframe. I knew immediately that the needed money for the DPO mother's burial cost would be met in only a matter of days.

The chaotic police side-duty continued at the station with a robbery suspect who insisted on seeing the State Commissioner of Police before he could make any confessional statement. This suspect had threatened to spill the beans if he was not connected immediately. A call was then put across to the Commissioner of Police, giving a detailed description of the suspect. A few minutes later, the DPO arrived at the station, and I overheard him assuring the suspect to cooperate as no harm would be meted out to him. Another call came through the walkie-talkie, though many of the spoken words were coded, I heard the voice say, "Give him VIP treatment".

The stupid robber proudly affirmed the order in ignorance. *"Yes! Better give me VIP treatment; I be one of Oga boys, "* he said in Pidgin English.

A few seconds after, I heard two gunshots fired and none of the policemen was startled; rather, all of them seemed to be in support of the shots – the robber was shot right there at the station. As the robber's body was being dragged away, I saw two cops sit together to draft a report that the robber died of the gunshots he suffered in an exchange of gunfire with the police. I never heard the voice of the suspect again; it was an open secret that he was silenced, just like that.

The police had silenced many people like that in the past without trial. These extra-judicial killings scared the living daylight out of me. The thought of being killed like a fowl pummelled my soul – shocker, considering I did that to others. Sleep vanished from my eyes with my fresh understanding that the police cell was not a place for relaxation. Each time a flashlight was flashed in the dungeon, I would quickly adjust myself between the other stinky inmates, who were also afraid of the evil intentions of the men in black. Most times, as the older inmates told me, such calls by the police always led to the end of an individual. Whenever an inmate was taken out, especially one with a serious crime against the state dangling over his head like the sword of Damocles, everyone considered it to be his end. In such instance, soulful Christian tunes and dirge were sung in English and Efik or Ibibio languages, and farewell bid him amidst tears. Even thugs cry. At this rate, sorrow would cut us all into pieces; I thought. Six of the inmates had been taken like this, and till date, nothing had been heard from them again. There was a time when a relative of one of the taken came; the old woman was told that her son's case had been transferred to Abuja.

Finally, I was arraigned at the High Court in Calabar for cult activities and murder charges;

my first day there was quite funny. Words I had never heard were the words that the gentlemen of the jury kept churning out. These words were so well-pronounced that its awe filled the courtroom and confused my senses. I heard words like prosecutor, proconsul, adjournment, litigation, addendum, and the list go on. Some of the lawyers were saying, "members of the bench", "this great jury" and so on. Every now and then, I would be startled with phrases like "objection my lord", and the magistrate would reply, "objection over-ruled or sustained".

"What in the world was all that, and how does that help my case?" I thoughtfully wondered.

Many times, I would just sit there pondering the rationale behind their wig. Can't they conduct their litigation without adorning their heads with that miserable wig?

The second day of my arraignment was meant to be a more welcome relief for me. As I had been praying, hoping, and looking forward to, my defence lawyer told me that he would secure bail for me. However, the bail application almost took eternity on that day; the prosecution counsel had averred that the suspect – me, had a tendency of jumping bail, and as such, I should be remanded in police custody. Thus, my hopes were dashed as bail was denied me.

On the sixth day, when my case was called for hearing, I became apprehensive when two warders pushed me forward to be docked, and my legs refused to support me. I recalled how I used to bark orders, and things happened in my favour, and with that I began to imagine our hitmen around the courtroom. I gave orders, but this time the orders only remained in my head and could not go through my lips. Instinctively, I knew this was the end of the road for me; tears welled up my eyes, and indeed, I looked so terrible like something the cat dragged in. The courtroom was quiet except occasional sighing and hissing from the many faces that thronged the room. Documents were tendered by both the proconsul and the prosecution. And the usual grammar associated with such a high-profile case ensued. I felt it was not going to be an easy task for the prosecutor to establish a criminal case against me, although the onus was on him to prove the case beyond a reasonable doubt.

Besides, my defence counsel had assured me that the burden of proof would be difficult to establish in this case. It was common knowledge that a person could not be convicted on circumstantial evidence alone. Hence, my earlier confession at the Etinan Police Station on the morning of my arrest would not be admitted in the court since it was done under duress, threats, and intimidation. After so many hearings and arguments, the Judge was prayed to dismiss and strike out the case on the grounds of lack of evidence and gross abuse of defendant's fundamental human rights, which I was subjected to by the police.

However, when the day of judgment was finally fixed, and I still had not seen neither Capone nor any Black Scorpion member come to my rescue, although Terror got me the lawyer and paid the legal fees, I knew I was going to prison. As usual, I was to be remanded in the police custody until judgement. While leading me out of the court to the Black Maria, the policeman attached to me pushed me violently, even in handcuff, as if I would disappear from the scene. He held me by my jean trousers on the waist and shoved me around at will like I was a defiant child running wild. I climbed into the vehicle with much difficulty; my legs were badly hurt from much police brutalities at the station. In the Black maria, I peeped through the little hole in the scary truck and noticed that the vehicle had veered off toward another direction, different from the route to the police station that I was familiar with.

Then, the vehicle got on a bad road, full of potholes, and started wobbling, constantly knocking my head against the metal frames of the truck. After a long drive, I heard what sounded like a heavy gate being flung open, and I peeped through the hole and saw two prison guards standing on either side of the open gate. It dawned on me that this was the State Prison, where convicted criminals were held; I sat up straight, shocked and confused, looking questioningly at the police officers with me. The Judge did not say I should be taken to a state penitentiary but back to police custody. What then necessitated this turn of events? I wondered. When the doors were unlocked for me to get down, I refused to get out of the vehicle, rguing with them; they beat me down from it and dragged me into the building to process my documentation. Then, I was led down a long corridor with different cells that accommodated several hard-looking criminals to a narrow cell. I pushed back on getting to the cell, my fingers clutched the cell bars trying to resist entering.

The guards tackled me to the ground with some more beatings and threw me into the cell, slamming the gated door.

I spent the next five weeks in this hellhole waiting for my sentencing, and by this time, I had made some friends and also firmly established myself as a "respected" member of the prison. I finally got my day in court. There was not enough evidence to convict me for the murder charges against the Governor's son and nephew. But shockingly, I was convicted with enough proof for violent cult activities, and I was sentenced to five years with hard labour. And this time, the same police officers treated and drove me back like a lord to the state prisons in the Black Maria to start my sentence.

Two weeks into my five-year sentence, a letter from Nsa was delivered to me by one of the police officers through Capone's connections. In the letter, I learnt that the former Zonal Butcher's right-hand man, Belema, had secretly nursed a grievance against the Black Scorpions for not choosing him as Capone. Thus, he made a secret deal with the authorities and snitched on Capone, Terror, and I with convincing evidence of being part of the violent cult activities in school. With all competition and line of the order of promotion removed, he stood a better chance of becoming Capone. Thus, the massive, desperate hunt for the three of us. And he was the one who told the police where to find me – we shared information among ourselves.

The letter also said Capone had sneaked out to some African country to lay low for a while but would return when the dust settles; he would probably lose a year of school or get rusticated – he was in his final year. Terror, who's British born, had been sneaked off to the United Kingdom by his parents to continue his education there, hopefully as a better person; he always wanted to leave this country, but his parents had kept him in Etinan against his will.

Sadly, Etete was attacked and killed by the rival cult at the private hospital where he was receiving treatment; they were tipped off by Belema in his quest to eliminate all opposition. This news broke my heart in a million pieces; trembling, I tipped my chin up and bit hard on my lower lip, tempting it to end my anguish, hoping it would. A small stream of blood trickled from the bite I could not feel, and a cruel smile stretched out across my face. My frozen heart shifted as the image of my best friend lying dead on the bed in a pool of blood from the knife stab in his chest flashed through my mind, …as if taking his right hand wasn't evil enough. My eyes finally failed me, I wept uncontrollably for him, even as nothing but clear rage welled up in me for this unprovoked injustice, and worse still, the senseless betrayal of the trust of brotherhood.

"How could Belema be so greedy for the position that he would destroy his own; a brother bound to him by blood oath? Where was the power and bond of brotherhood that the Black Scorpion promised? How could the coffin be nailed on Etete …forever? We have lost so many lives amongst us, but again, we set the nails on our own coffins by the singular choice of cultism we made," I wept thoughtfully.

Belema played his tunes and made us all dance to it, but the thing about playing any tunes is that it also eventually pulls the player to dance to its rhythms. As Belema had planned, he became Capone. Being left with no other option and having not learnt the truth, the Zonal Godfather initiated him the following night after I was sentenced. But I also know the nails on his coffin are set, unless Capone – Etim Nkanta, is not the man I know him to be.

Epilogue

When I was being driven back to the state prison after my sentencing, I realised I would get out of jail two years after my course mates had graduated from the university. Such a waste of years and so much for all the troubles to gain admission into the university. I needed to distract myself from this painful reality, so, while walking into the premises and down the long corridor, I focused on several inscriptions on the prison walls. The names of past and present heads of state in Nigeria dotted one side of the wall, and the names of despotic African rulers were visible on the opposite side of the wall. I saw names like Mobutu Sese Seko, Idi Amin Dada, Jean-Bédel Bokassa, Laurent Kabila, Maumur Gaddafi, and Sani Abacha. Then, on the side of the wall opposite the prison gate, which served as the only entry and exit, there were names of human rights and civil right activists from all over the world: Martin Luther King Jnr, Gani Fawehinmi, Malcolm X, Nelson Mandela, Ken Saro-Wiwa, Che Guevara, and Steve Biko. However, what I was yet to decipher was what these names meant to inmates of this prison.

Well, none of the writings impressed me at all except the old Christian song *"I surrender all"*, which was conspicuously written vertically on the slim wall before my cell. I guess that got my attention because it spoke to my current predicament; without any hope of rescue from my guys, I had surrendered all to this hellhole. The inscription also reinforced the words of the leader in a Church I had visited in my disguise while hiding from the law. But it also aroused an uncanny desire in me to repent of my evil deeds. A pocket Bible, which was used for the prison morning devotions, helped to strengthen my resolve to serve the Almighty God. I took it and randomly opened to *Matthew 7:7* and read it to myself. The words intrigued me, and with that, another desire for an Informinua was strongly ingrained on my mind; this time, I wanted to inform him about the kingdom of God, not him inform me about the rival cults. Was that even possible? I wondered, smiling at my thoughts.

I am irrelevant in the scheme of things right now; unable to help myself. But I know there has to be a way out; so, all I have is hope.

Your brother,
Anietie

Glossary

Abi: Pidgin English (Nigerian) word for affirming or questioning something.

Afang: Vegetable used for cooking soup in the southern part of Nigeria by the people of Efik, Ibibio and Igbo ethnic groups.

Alalok: A commercial motor-cyclist in Akwa Ibom and Cross River State, Nigeria.

APC: Armoured Personnel Carrier.

ASUU: Academic Staff Union of Universities.

Belong: To be a member of any clandestine group, especially secret organisation in the university.

Bone: To shun, forget or ignore anyone, place and thing.

dolapo: A slang that means dullard, borrowed form the Yoruba language in Nigeria.

D.P.O: Divisional Police Officer.

Eyen-Isong: translated as son of the soil by Efik/Ibibio speaking group.

Eba: Pulverised garri which is prepared by adding hot water to it.

Hell item: Means to sell something.

Igbo: Another name for Marijuana in Nigeria.

Ikong-Ekpo: the meaning of marijuana in Ibibio language.

I.P.O: Investigating Police Officer.

274

Informinua: An informant for the cult group. It's coined from a combination of the two words: information and *inua* (means mouth in Efik/Ibibio language).

Jew-men: this describes cowards and non-members of the secret cult society in tertiary institution.

Lepa: this is a Yoruba slang used to describe a slender person.

Legsus: Nigerian slang for trekking, coined from the Lexus car.

Mugu: Nigerian slang that means a fool, borrowed from the Hausa language.

Mumu: means a fool in Nigerian Pidgin English that suggests somebody is worse than a fool.

NEPA: National Electric Power Authority.

NASU: Non-Academic Staff Union.

Obtain: To get something from somebody through force and clever means.

Oga: A slang used for an senior persons, a boss, a wealthy person, or an officer of the law.

Ogogoro: A locally brewed Gin.

Pepper: A slang often used to mean money or wealth.

Runz: Businesses or illegal activities aimed at gaining undue advantage and cutting due process.

SSANU: Senior Staff Association of Nigerian Universities.

Shack: Drinking alcoholic liquor to a point of intoxication; it also means to drink any liquid.

SUG: Students Union Government.

Toasting: this is a slang for the act of engaging a member of the opposite sex for a relationship. Young men guilty of this are called **Toaster.**

Useme: This is an Ibibio word which means stupid or moron (zombie).

Woh-woh: This means an ugly person.

www.ingramcontent.com/pod-product-compliance
Lightning Source LLC
Chambersburg PA
CBHW030117180626
46812CB00002B/453